LOVING
SABOTAGE

LOVING SABOTAGE

AMÉLIE NOTHOMB

WITH AN AFTERWORD
BY THE AUTHOR

TRANSLATED BY ANDREW WILSON

A NEW DIRECTIONS BOOK

Originally published in France by Éditions Albin Michel, Paris, with the title
Le sabotage amoureux in 1993. Published by arrangement with Éditions Albin
Michel, Paris, and Hurricane Press, Vancouver, B.C., Canada.

TRANSLATOR'S ACKNOWLEDGMENTS
The translator thanks Kevin Cook of Nijmegen for expert advice (mostly but
not always taken) on bridging languages and cultures, and for ongoing friendship; Barbara Tessman of Toronto for expert advice on matters editorial
(almost entirely taken) and for even longer ongoing friendship; Françoise
Venturelli of Véraz and Geneva for her patient teaching and passionate
defense of the French language; Chuck Kim of New York for his enthusiasm
and guidance on matters of intellectual property and international publishing;
and most of all, Amélie Nothomb for writing this delightful book.

The Publisher would also like to thank The French Publishers Agency, New
York, for its assistance.

Manufactured in the United States of America
New Directions Books are printed on acid-free paper.
First published as New Directions Paperbook 31 (NDP31) in 2008
Interior and jacket designed by Sylvia Frezzolini Severance

Library of Congress Cataloging-in-Publication Data

Nothomb, Amélie
    [Sabotage amoureux. English]
    Loving sabotage/by Amélie Nothomb ; with an afterword by the author.
        p. cm.
    "A New Directions Book."
    ISBN 13: 978-0-8112-1782-8
    I. Title.
PQ2674.O778 S2313 2000
843'.914—dc21   00-055025

New Directions Books are published for James Laughlin
by New Directions Publishing Corporation
80 Eighth Avenue, New York 10011

LOVING SABOTAGE

With a great thundering of hooves, I galloped among the electric fans.

I was seven years old. Nothing in the world felt as good as my brain filled to overflowing with oxygen. The faster I galloped, the more the air rushed in and pushed everything else out.

My horse surged onto the Square of the Great Fan, more commonly known as Tiananmen Square. Then he veered right, onto the Boulevard of Habitable Ugliness.

With one hand I held his reins. The other was fully occupied with expressing the vastness within me, stroking in turn my horse's rump and the sky above Peking. The pedestrians, the spittle on the ground, the donkeys, and the electric fans — all faded away before my mounted elegance.

No need to put spur to this horse. China had created him in my image: the essence of speed and grandeur, a roaring engine stoked by the admiration of the crowd.

From my first day in China, the axiom had been clear to me: In the City of Electric Fans, all that is not splendid is hideous.

Which is to say that almost everything was hideous.

Which imposed an immediate corollary: The splendor of the world was me.

Not my seven years of skin, of flesh, of hair and bone; I knew they were nothing compared with the fabulous creatures of the *Arabian Nights*, or those in the international ghetto.

No, the splendor of the world was the elegant dance I offered to the day; it was the fleetness of my horse; it was my forehead cresting like a sail before the breezes of the electric fans.

Peking smelled like baby's vomit. All along the Boulevard of Habitable Ugliness, only my drumming hoofbeats countered the hacking gargle of throats being cleared, the prohibition against contact with the Chinese, and the awful emptiness of the gazes.

As we approached the ghetto's perimeter, my steed slowed to allow the guards to identify me. Apparently I looked no more suspicious to them today than on any other day.

I rode into the heart of the ghetto of San Li Tun, where I had lived since the invention of writing. Which is to say for about two years — roughly speaking during the Neolithic era, the regime of the Gang of Four.

"The world is all that is the case," wrote Wittgenstein in his admirable prose.

In 1974, Peking was not the case: I don't know how else to describe the situation.

Wittgenstein was not my preferred reading when I was seven. Yet I had already arrived at the above concept through my own observations, and concluded that Peking and the world had little to do with each other.

Still, I had accommodated myself to it. I had a horse, and a brain bubbling over with oxygen. In fact, I had everything. I was an epic unto myself. I felt kinship only with the Great Wall, the single human construction visible from the moon. At least it respected my scale. Far from enclosing my vision, the Wall drew it towards infinity.

Each morning, a slave arrived to do my hair.

She didn't know she was my slave. She thought she was Chinese. In truth, however, she had no nationality, since she was my slave.

Before Peking, I lived in Japan, where the best slaves were found. The quality of slaves in China left much to be desired.

In Japan, at the age of four I'd had a slave devoted

3

to me alone. She frequently prostrated herself at my feet. That was as it should be.

The Peking slave had no knowledge of such refinements. She began each morning by combing my long hair, a job she attacked like a mindless brute. I yelled with pain and in my mind flogged her mercilessly. Next, she wove my tresses into one or two admirable braids, the Cultural Revolution not having diminished the ancestral art of the pigtail by even a hair. I much preferred her to fashion a single braid; it seemed more appropriate to a person of my rank.

This Chinese was called Trê, a name I found unacceptable. I let her know that she would bear the charming name of my Japanese slave. She stared at me vacantly and continued to call herself Trê. From that day on, I understood that something was rotten in the politics of this country.

Some countries are like drugs. This is certainly the case with China, with its astonishing power to make all who have been there pretentious — even those who simply talk about the place.

Pretentiousness compels people to write. Witness the extraordinary number of books about China. In keeping with the country itself, these works are either the best (Leys, Segalen, Claudel) or the worst.

I was no exception to the rule. China made me very pretentious indeed. But I had an excuse that few minor sinologists can claim: I was five when I arrived and eight when I left. I remember very well the day I learned that I was going to live in China. I was only five, but already I understood the essential part, which was that I would be able to boast about it.

This is a rule with no exceptions: even China's greatest critics look forward as enthusiastically to setting foot there as they would to the offer of a knighthood.

Nothing inflates a person's importance so much as the casually uttered words, "I've just come back from China." Even today, when I feel I'm not being treated with due admiration, I'll drop an indifferent sounding "When I lived in Peking. . . ."

This has something concrete and specific to it; after all, I could also say, "When I lived in Laos," which would clearly be more exceptional. But it is less chic. China is the classic, the unconditional, the Chanel No. 5.

And yet, simple snobbery cannot provide the full explanation. Fantasy also plays an enormous and undeniable role. The traveller who disembarks in China without a goodly dose of illusions about the place will never see anything but a nightmare.

My mother always had the happiest temperament in the universe. The night of our arrival in Peking, the sheer ugliness struck her so strongly that she wept. And this was a woman who never wept.

Of course it also had the Forbidden City, the Temple of Heaven, the Perfumed Mountain, the Great Wall, the Ming Tombs. But they were for Sunday. The

5

rest of the week featured only filth, hopelessness, unending concrete, the ghetto and surveillance — all disciplines in which the Chinese excel.

No other country blinds one so thoroughly: everyone who has been there speaks of the splendors they have seen. Even the best-intentioned tend not to mention the creeping hideousness that could not have escaped them. It is a strange phenomenon. China is like a skillful courtesan who manages to make her innumerable physical imperfections disappear without even hiding them, and who infatuates all her lovers.

Two years earlier, my father had received the news of his re-assignment to Peking with a solemn face.

I didn't see how we could think of leaving the village of Shukugawa, the mountains, our house and our garden.

My father explained that the problem wasn't what we were leaving but where we were going. China, he indicated, was a country in which all was not well.

"Are they having a war?" I asked hopefully.

"No."

I sulked. They were making me leave my beloved Japan for a country that wasn't even at war. True, it was China; that had a good sound to it. But how would Japan get along without me? The ministry's lack of forethought was disturbing.

In 1972 our departure drew close. The situation was tense. My teddy bears were packed. I heard someone say that China was a communist country. I resolved to analyze that. But there were more immediate worries: the house was being emptied. One day there was nothing left. It was time to leave.

Peking airport: without a doubt, this is another country.

For some obscure reason, our luggage has not arrived with us. We will have to wait at the airport for several hours till it arrives. How many hours? Perhaps two, perhaps four, perhaps twenty-four. One of China's charms is its unpredictability.

Very well. This gives me time to begin my analysis of the situation. I wander through the airport with an inquisitive air. They were right: this country is very different. I can't tell exactly what this difference entails. True, it is ugly, but with a kind of ugliness I've never seen before. There must be a word to define this ugliness, but I don't know it yet.

I ask myself just what communism might be. I am five years old, and it is far beneath my dignity to ask an adult what the word means. After all, I didn't need their assistance to learn to speak. If I'd had to ask them every time I wanted a definition, I'd still be at the babbling stage. I learned by myself that dog meant dog, that bad meant bad: I see no reason to ask for help with one more word.

Besides, it shouldn't be difficult. There is something very specific here. I ask myself what it involves. There are the people, who all dress the same. There is the light, which is the same as the light in the Kobe Hospital. There is . . .

Careful, now. Communism is here, certainly, but let's not give it a meaning so lightly. It is a word, and therefore important. What, therefore, is the strangest thing about this place?

Suddenly the question exhausts me. I lie down on one of the airport's huge tiles and fall asleep.

I wake up. I don't know how many hours I've slept. My parents are still waiting for our luggage, fatigue on their faces. My brother and sister are asleep on the floor.

I have forgotten about communism. I'm thirsty. My father gives me a little money to buy myself something to drink.

I wander around. There don't seem to be any colored soft drinks as one finds in Japan. All they sell is tea. "China is a country where tea is drunk," I say to myself. Okay. I walk up to the little old man who sells it. He hands me a bowl of steaming tea.

I sit on the floor with the enormous bowl. The tea is fabulous. I have never had its equal. In a few seconds my brain is drunk with it and I have the first high of my life. I love it. I am going to do great things in this country.

I skip across the airport, spinning like a top.

And at that instant, I come nose to nose with communism.

It is pitch black outside when the baggage finally arrives.

A car takes us across a bizarre world. It is almost midnight, and the streets are broad and deserted.

My parents still look exhausted. My older siblings gaze about them with astonishment.

The hit of caffeine is launching fireworks in my brain. I give no sign, but I am crazed with excitement. Everything seems awesome, especially me. Ideas play hopscotch in my head.

I have no awareness that my ecstasy is inappropriate to the situation. I am out of sync with the Gang of Four's China. And will be so for the next three years.

The car arrives at the ghetto of San Li Tun. The ghetto is surrounded by high walls, and the walls are surrounded by soldiers. The buildings resemble prison blocks. We have been assigned a fourth-floor apartment. There is no elevator, and the eight flights of stairs run with streamlets of urine.

We carry our baggage up. My mother weeps. I sense that it would not be a good idea to share my euphoria. I keep it to myself.

From the window of my new bedroom, China is

hilariously ugly. I give the sky a condescending glance. I bounce up and down on the bed.

"The world is all that is the case," wrote Wittgenstein.

According to the Chinese newspapers, all sorts of edifying things were the case in Peking.

None of them were verifiable.

Every week, the diplomatic bags brought foreign papers to the embassies: the articles about China seemed to describe another planet.

A limited-circulation newsletter was distributed to the members of the Chinese government and, through some aberrant concern for transparency, to foreign diplomats. It came from the same organization as *The People's Daily* and its news items had nothing to do with anything. The articles were so lacking in triumphalism that they might have been true, but their accuracy could not be assumed; under the Gang of Four, the fabricators of succeeding editions often got tangled up in their own misinformation.

This made things difficult for the foreign community. Many diplomats said that, at the end of the day, they had no idea what was going on in China.

Not surprisingly, the reports that they had to write to their respective ministries were the most polished and literary of their careers. One need search no further to explain the number of writers who found their vocation in Peking.

Had Baudelaire known that "Anywhere out of the world" would someday emerge in China's profusion of true, false, and neither-true-nor-false, he would not have wished for it so ardently.

In 1974, I read neither Wittgenstein nor Baudelaire nor even *The People's Daily*.

I read very little: I had far too much to do. Reading was fine for those underemployed creatures, the adults. They had to find something to occupy themselves.

As for me, I had important functions to attend to.

I had a horse that took three-quarters of my time.

I had crowds to awe.

I had a public image to maintain.

I had a legend to build.

And above all, there was the war: the terrible, epic war of the ghetto of San Li Tun.

Take a crowd of children of various nationalities, enclose them in a restricted space built of concrete, and then let them loose, without supervision. Anyone who thinks the kids will extend the hand of friendship to each other is an idiot.

My family's arrival coincided with an international summit at which it was declared that the outcome of the Second World War had been mishandled in the haste of the moment. The whole thing had to be refought, but the essential remained: the Germans were still the Bad Guys.

11

And there was no shortage of Germans in San Li Tun.

Also, the world war had lacked amplitude: this time, the Allied forces included all possible nationalities, even the Chileans and the Cameroonians.

But not the Americans, and not the British.

Racism? No, geography. The war was limited to the ghetto of San Li Tun. It happened that the British lived in the ancient ghetto called Wai Jiao Ta Lu. As for the Americans, they all lived in their own special compound, gathered around their ambassador, one George Bush.

The absence of these two nations did not disturb us in the least. We could do without the Americans and the British. But not the Germans.

The war began in 1972. That was the year I awoke to a profound truth: no one on this earth is indispensable, except the enemy.

Without an enemy, human beings are poor things indeed. Their lives are ordeals, crushed between insignificance and boredom.

The enemy is the Savior. His mere existence is enough to revitalize humanity. Thanks to the enemy, that unfortunate accident called life becomes an epic.

Clearly, Christ was right to have said, "Love thine enemy." Unfortunately, he then formulated some absurd corollaries from this: making peace, turning the other cheek, etc.

What nonsense! If one makes peace with one's enemy, he ceases to be an enemy. And if one is left without an enemy, one is obliged to search for another. Which is to start all over again.

Which is to have gotten nowhere.

Therefore: one must love one's enemy, but not tell him so. And one must absolutely avoid making peace.

Armistice is a luxury that human beings cannot afford. Proof can be seen in the fact that all periods of peace end in war. Whereas wars generally end in periods of peace.

From which we may deduce that peace is harmful, while war is beneficial.

Ergo, we must accept war's occasional inconveniences philosophically.

Not one newspaper, not one press agency, not one historian has ever mentioned the world war of the San Li Tun ghetto, which lasted from 1972 till 1975. With some confidence, I can say that my early years gave me a firm grounding in censorship and misinformation.

How can a war that lasted three years, involved dozens of nations, and witnessed horrible atrocities, simply be ignored?

The media's pretext for their silence? The average age of the combatants was approximately ten. Could it really be that children have no place in History?

Shortly after the international summit of 1972, some informer tipped off the adults about the war that was about to commence.

The parents accepted that bellicose tension was so strong that they could not prevent the imminent conflict. However, a new war against the Germans risked unacceptable repercussions with the Teutonic adults. In Peking, the non-communist countries had to stick together.

A parental delegation therefore issued its conditions: "Yes to world war, given that it is inevitable. But no West German may be declared an enemy."

This clause didn't bother us in the least. There were more than enough East Germans to serve our purposes.

But the adults wanted more: they required that the West Germans be incorporated into the Allied forces. This we could not accommodate. We were prepared not to beat them up, but to welcome them as comrades-in-arms seemed to us unnatural. In any case, the West German children drew little comfort from their non-combatant status. Lacking an enemy, the poor things languished in neutrality, bored stiff.

(The exceptions were a few traitors who defected to the Eastern Bloc — another shameful fact that has been hushed up.)

Thus, in the minds of the grown-ups, the situation had been normalized: the children's war was now a war against communism. I can attest, however, that this was never the case from the children's point of view. For the role of the Bad Guys, only the Germans excited any enthusiasm among us. The proof can be seen in our never having fought the Albanians, Bulgarians, or other minor nationalities of San Li Tun. These negligible quantities stayed out of play.

As to the Russians, the question never arose: they too had their own compound. The other Eastern Bloc countries were quartered in Wai Jiao Ta Lu, with the exception of the Yugoslavs (whom we had no reason to cast as enemies) and the Rumanians (whom the adults obliged us to enroll in our cause, it being fashionable to have Rumanian friends in that era).

These were the only adult interventions in our declaration of war. I must emphasize how artificial they seemed to us.

I was, at seven, the youngest member of the Allies in 1974. The eldest, who was thirteen, seemed to me almost geriatric. The core of our forces were French, but the best-represented continent was Africa: Cameroonians, Malians, Zairians, Moroccans, Algerians, etc. swelled our battalions. There were also Chileans, Italians, and those aforementioned Rumanians, whom we couldn't stand because they had been imposed on us and because they always acted like some official delegation.

The Belgians were limited to three: my brother André, my sister Juliette, and me. There were no other children of our nationality. In 1975 two beautiful little Flemish girls arrived, but they were hopeless pacifists: we could do nothing with them.

Beginning in 1972, in the very heart of the army, a

nucleus of three countries was formed which proved as faithful in friendship as in combat: the French, the Belgians, and the Cameroonians. The last had impossible first names, loud voices, and laughed all the time: we adored them. The French seemed picturesque to us: they asked us in all seriousness to say things in Belgian, which made us giggle, and they often mentioned someone whose surname — Pompidou — I found hilarious.

The Italians were either the best or the worst: their number included as many cowards as heroes. And even then, the valor of the latter depended on their mood. The bravest among them could turn into a complete coward the day after performing some prodigious exploit. Their contingent included a half-Italian, half-Egyptian girl named Jihan: at the age of twelve, she stood 5 foot 7 and weighed 150 pounds. This gargantua was a formidable military asset. Alone, she could force the retreat of a German patrol, and it was spectacular to watch that huge body lashing about. But her amazing growth put her personality out of whack. On the days that Jihan was growing, she was undeployable and unbearable.

The Zairians were marvellous fighters: the problem was that they battled each other as much as they fought the enemy. And if we intervened in their internecine quarrels, they fought us as well.

◆

The war rapidly took on serious proportions, and it became clear that our army required a hospital.

In the heart of the ghetto, near the brick factory, we found a huge moving crate. It was large enough for ten of us to stand in it. This wooden crate was unanimously adopted as our military hospital.

However, hospitals require staff. My sister Juliette, aged ten, was declared too pretty and too delicate for frontline duty. She was appointed nurse/doctor/surgeon/psychiatrist/attendant, and carried out these duties marvelously. From the Swiss (who had a reputation for hygiene) she pilfered a supply of sterile gauze, ointment, aspirin, and vitamin C — she deemed the latter to be an outstanding remedy for faint-heartedness.

During an expedition deep into enemy territory, our forces managed to take the garage of one of the East German families. Garages were positions of considerable strategic importance, because that was where adults stored their provisions. And God knows, such stocks were precious in Peking, where the markets sold little more than pork and cabbage.

In the Teutonic garage, we unearthed a case full of powdered soup packets. These were confiscated and transported to the hospital. That left us with the task of finding a use for them. A study group deliberated on the question and discovered that the soup tasted much better in its powdered state. Our generals met secretly with the nurse/doctor and decreed that the powder would be our warrior's tonic; we attributed to it healing powers not only for physical wounds but for ailments of the soul as well. Anyone caught mixing it with water would be court-martialled.

The tonic was such a success that the hospital was always full. Malingerers could be forgiven: Juliette had transformed it from a dispensary to an antechamber of Eden. She made the "sick" and the "wounded" comfortable on mattresses of *The People's Daily*, she questioned them with gentle gravity about their suffering, she sang them lullabies, and fanned them while pouring the contents of a soup packet into their open mouths. Nirvana could not have provided so agreeable a sojourn.

Our generals suspected the true nature of these epidemics but took no disciplinary action. After all, it seemed good for troop morale and netted the army a number of unsolicited recruits — though undeniably, the new soldiers joined up in hopes of being wounded. The generals weren't unhappy so long as valiant warriors could be made of them.

It took some perseverance for me to be admitted to the Allied ranks. They said I was too small. There were others of my age and younger in the ghetto, but none yet had any military ambition.

I argued my merits: courage, tenacity, fierce loyalty, and above all my speed on horseback.

This last virtue caught their attention.

The generals debated at length among themselves

and at last summoned me before them. I arrived trembling. They announced that, given my small size and my speed, I had been appointed an army pathfinder.

"Besides, since you're still a baby, the enemy will never suspect you."

The slight did not dampen my joy in my new rank in the least.

Pathfinder! I could not conceive of anything grander, more beautiful, or more fitting. It was a word I could seize from one end to the other, in all its senses. I could ride it like a mustang, hang from it as if from a trapeze: from any angle I approached the word, it was beautiful.

The survival of the entire army depends on the pathfinder. Risking her life, she advances alone to locate the hazards in unknown territory. The slightest twist of fate could see her tread on a mine and be blown to smithereens — her body a heroic jigsaw puzzle, rising above the earth in a mushroom cloud of human confetti — and her comrades in their bivouacs, seeing the organic fragments scattered across the heavens, would cry, "The pathfinder!" After soaring skyward in a trajectory befitting their historic importance, the pieces would hang for a moment in the ether, then return to earth with such grace that even the enemy would weep at so a noble sacrifice. I dreamed of dying thus, such pyrotechnics rendering my legend eternal.

The pathfinder's mission is to find the way, in all meanings of the term. Finding the way — this mission fit me like a glove. I would blaze like a human torch or, in a contradictory stroke of Protean genius, become invisible and inaudible, my furtive silhouette slipping unnoticed among the enemy ranks. The picaresque spy disguises himself; the epic pathfinder does not stoop to such travesty. Cloaked in shadow, she nobly risks her life.

And when, after some suicide reconnaissance mission, the pathfinder returns to base, her army — awestruck with gratitude — receives her information as if it were manna from heaven. From the moment she opens her mouth to speak, the generals hang on every word. No one congratulates her, but everyone casts direct and glowing looks at her that say so much more.

In all my life, never has a position satisfied me so much as that one: no title has so profoundly suited my sense of self.

Later in life, when I had achieved either martyrdom or a Nobel Prize in medicine, I would accept these slightly shopworn honors without too much disappointment. For I could always remind myself that while the noblest part of my existence was behind me, it was mine forever. Till my death, I would be able to awe people with the simple sentence: "During the war, I was a pathfinder in Peking."

Were I to read Ho Chi Minh in the original, translate Marx into classical Hittite, undertake a stylistic analysis of the epanodoses of the *Little Red Book*, carry out an oulipian transcription of the thoughts of Lenin; were I to sacrifice communism on the altar of my analysis, or vice versa; even so, I will never surpass my analytical achievements as a five-year-old.

I had scarcely set foot on Red soil, or even left the airport, and already I understood.

I had found the only vector permitting the situation to be summed up in a single sentence.

This statement was simultaneously beautiful, simple, poetic and, in the manner of all the great verities, a little disappointing.

"Water boils at 100 degrees centigrade." Behold the elemental beauty of that phrase, which yet leaves one slightly unsatisfied.

But real beauty must leave one unsatisfied; it must leave the soul a measure of desire.

In this way, my sentence was beautiful.

Here it is: "A communist country is one in which there are electric fans."

This sentence is so structurally luminous that it could serve perfectly as an example in a Viennese treatise on logic. Yet its stylistic graces aside, the statement is remarkable in that it is true.

When I found myself nose to nose with a bouquet of electric fans in Peking airport, this truth struck me with the inexplicable force of a revelation.

These strange blooms, their revolving petals surrounded by salad colanders, could only be evidence of an extraordinary environment.

Japan had been air conditioned. I could not remember ever seeing these plastic vegetables there.

Air conditioning did sometimes exist in communist countries, but it never worked; therefore, electric fans were necessary.

Later on I lived in two other communist countries, Burma and Laos, which confirmed my observations of 1972.

I am not saying that there are no electric fans in non-communist countries, but they are less pervasive, and, more subtly, they are of no significance.

The electric fan is to communism as the epithet is to Homer: Homer is not the only writer in the world to employ epithets, but it was under his pen that the epithet took on its full meaning.

In his 1985 film *While Father Was Away on Business*, Kusturica shot a scene about a communist interrogation which presented three characters : the interrogator, the interrogated, and an electric fan. During the interminable question and answer, the swivelling head of the machine stops, accordingly to some inexorable rhythm, sometimes facing the interrogator, sometimes the man he is interrogating; it freezes on one person before sweeping back to the other. The absurd and exasperating movement carries the scene to its climax.

All through the interrogation, nothing moves — not the two men, not even the camera. There is only the oscillation of the electric fan. Without it, the scene would never achieve such a degree of tension. The fan plays the role of Greek chorus, but far more intolerably because it passes no sentences, thinks nothing, is content to add resonance to the scene and carry out, with infallible exactitude, its job as an electric fan: efficient and disinterested, the ideal chorus of all totalitarian regimes.

I doubt that even the approval of a famous Yugoslav film maker will convince readers of the pertinence of my reflections on electric fans. No matter. Is anyone still so naive as to imagine that theories are meant to be believed? Theories serve to annoy philistines, appeal to aesthetes, and amuse the rest of us.

The essential mission of a confounding verity is to defy analysis. Take Vialatte's marvellous sentence: "July is a very monthly month." Has anything more true and more confounding ever been said about the month of July?

Today, I no longer live in Peking and I no longer own a horse. I have exchanged Peking for blank paper and the horse for ink. My heroism has gone underground.

I always knew that adulthood didn't count; following puberty, all existence is but epilogue.

In Peking, my life was of capital importance. Humanity needed me.

Besides, I was a pathfinder, and the world was at war.

Our army had found a new form of aggression against the enemy.

Every morning, the Chinese authorities delivered plain yogurt to the inhabitants of the ghetto. They placed at the door of each apartment a small box containing individual portions of yogurt in glass bottles, each topped by a flimsy paper lid. The white yogurt was covered by a layer of yellowish whey.

At dawn, a raiding party of male soldiers assembled before the doors of the East German apartments, raised the paper lids, drank the whey and replaced it with an equivalent measure of similar-colored liquid from their own bodies. Unseen, they replaced the lids and stole away.

We never knew if our victims ate their yogurt. It seems very likely, since no complaint was ever raised. The Chinese yogurt was so acidic that certain odd flavors might very well have passed unnoticed.

The villainy of this deed left us squirming with delight. We told ourselves we were disgusting. It was superb.

The East German children were sturdy, courageous, and strong. The worst they ever did was beat us up. This form of aggression seemed pathetic compared with our crimes.

We were ingenious little beasts. The sum of our army's muscles was ludicrous measured against that of the enemy forces, even though they were less numerous. But we were far nastier.

Whenever one of us fell into the hands of the East Germans, he or she was released an hour later covered in bumps and bruises.

When the opposite occurred, the enemy got it back in spades.

To begin with, our ministrations took much longer. The young German was treated to at least an afternoon's worth of amusements. Sometimes considerably more.

With the victim looking on, we began by indulging in an intellectual orgy regarding his fate. As we spoke in French, the Teuton understood nothing, which only increased his apprehension — especially since our suggestions were delivered with such glee and cruel passion that our faces and voice provided excellent subtitles. Understatement was beneath our dignity:

"We'll cut off his ___ and both of his ___" served as the classic preamble to our verbal pile-on.

(There were no girls among the East Germans, a mystery to which I've never found the key. Perhaps the parents left them in their native land, in the hands of some swimming coach or weightlifting trainer.)

"With Mr. Chang's kitchen knife."

"No! With Mr. Ziegler's razor."

"And we'll make him eat it," declared a pragmatist, to whom the ways and means were of secondary importance.

"With his ___ and his ___ for seasoning."

25

"Nice and slowly," added a lover of adverbs.

"Yes, he'll have to really chew," said a glossarial soul.

"And afterwards, we'll make him puke them back up," proffered a blasphemer.

"Nah! That's what he'd be hoping for. It has to stay in his stomach," asserted someone with a sense of the sacred.

"Even if we have to block up his ___, so it never comes out," added a comrade who could envision the long term.

"Yes," spake a disciple of Saint Matthew.

"It won't work," commented a philistine, whom everyone ignored.

"With builder's cement. And we'll block up his mouth too, so he can't call for help."

"We'll block *everything* up!" exalted a mystic.

"Chinese cement is shit," opined an expert.

"So much the better. That way, he'll be blocked up with shit," resumed the mystic, now in a trance.

"But that will kill him," stammered a sissy who imagined himself to be the Geneva Convention.

"No," spake the disciple of Saint Matthew.

"We won't let him die. That would be too easy."

"He must suffer till the end!"

"What end?" enquired the Geneva Convention.

"You know, when it's all over. When we let him run crying to his Mommy."

"I can just imagine her, when she sees how we've redecorated her dirty little brat!"

"That'll teach her to have German babies!"

"The only good Germans are Germans blocked up with Chinese cement."

This aphorism, sufficiently cryptic to excite general enthusiasm, raised a howl from the assembly.

"Okay. But before that, we have to pull out his hair and his eyebrows and his eyelashes."

"And his fingernails!"

"We'll pull everything off!" intoned the mystic.

"And we'll mix it with cement before we block him up."

"That'll give him something to remember us by."

These exercises in style were a little pathetic because we fairly quickly ran into the limits of language, especially since we captured victims quite often. It required stellar imaginations to keep topping the threats without diluting them.

The body being less vast than the language, we explored the latter with an ardor that would have given a lesson to lexicographers:

"Hey, those are also called testicles."

"Or gonads."

"Or just plain nuts."

"Look, here's a nutcracker!"

"Put it away — you don't crack peanuts! You just pull the shells off . . . "

I was the one who said least during these verbal tournaments, in which the phrases bounced from one voice to another like shuttlecocks in a badminton game. I listened entranced by such eloquence and audacity in the service of Evil.

The orators reminded me of a group of jugglers, displaying their virtuosity until some blockhead dropped one of the balls. So I preferred to stay out of the game and simply follow the multiple trajectories of the conversation. Only by myself would I speak, playing with my sentences like a sea lion, bouncing them from the end of my nose like a red balloon.

The poor German kid had plenty of opportunity to wet his pants by the time our army finally moved from theory to practice. He'd listened to the menacing laughter and the verbal strafing. Often he wept in fear as the executioners approached, to our great delight:

"Sissy!"

"Gonad!"

Alas, such is the tragedy of language — deeds fell short of words. The actual torture featured very little diversity.

In general, it was limited to dunking in the Secret Weapon.

Among other ingredients, the Secret Weapon was composed of everyone's urine, with the exception of that reserved for the German yogurt. With exemplary zeal, we never voided our precious liquid anywhere but in our large wash basin. The latter was kept atop the fire escape of the ghetto's highest building, and guarded by our toughest soldiers.

(For ages, the adults and other spectators wondered why they so often saw children rushing towards that fire escape in obvious agitation.)

To this decreasingly fresh urine we added a goodly proportion of Indian ink.

The result of this simple chemical formula was a greenish elixir with an ammoniacal fragrance.

The German was grabbed by the arms and legs, and submerged in the tub.

After that, we disposed of the Secret Weapon, on the grounds that the victim had contaminated its monstrous purity. And we began again to bank our urine for the next prisoner.

If I had read Wittgenstein at that time, I would have found him beside the point.

Six abstruse propositions to explain the world, when one — and such a simple one at that — would have covered the entire system!

And I didn't have to think about it to discover it, nor formulate it in order to live it. It was an acquired certitude. It was born with me every morning:

"The universe exists so that I can exist."

My parents, communism, cotton dresses, the *Tales of the Arabian Nights,* yogurt, the diplomatic corps, enemies, the odor of brickmaking, the right-angle, ice skates, Chou Enlai, spelling, and the Boulevard of Habitable Ugliness: none of this was superfluous since it all existed in relation to my existence.

All roads led to me.

China's sin was excess of modesty. The Middle Kingdom? One need only hear that term to understand its limits. China was the middle of the planet only insofar as it stayed put.

Whereas I could go wherever I wanted: the world's center of gravity followed in my wake.

Among other things, nobility means accepting the obvious. Why deny that the world had been preparing for my existence for billions of years?

The question of post-me occupied my thoughts but little. Without a doubt, a few additional billions of years would be required for the last essayists to finish their commentaries on me. But this was hardly important, given the dizzying immediacy of my days. I left these speculations to my commentarists, and to my commentarists' commentarists.

Thus, Wittgenstein was beside the point. And he had committed a grave error: he had written. He might as well have given up right then.

As long as the Chinese emperors didn't write, China was at its zenith. Decadence began with the first imperial writings.

Myself, I didn't write. When one has giant fans to impress, when one has a horse to ride at an intoxicating gallop, when one has an army whose path needs finding, when one has a rank to maintain and an enemy to humiliate, one keeps one's head high and does not write.

◆

Nonetheless, it was in the heart of the City of Electric Fans that my decadence began.

It commenced the moment I realized that I was not the center of the world. The moment I discovered, to my astonishment, who the center of the world actually was.

In the summertime I went about barefoot. No self-respecting pathfinder ever wears shoes. My footsteps in the ghetto made as little noise as *tai chi*, a forbidden discipline at the time but still practiced in terrified silence by a few enthusiasts.

Furtively, solemnly, I sought out the enemy.

San Li Tun was such an ugly place that one needed a continuing epic in order to survive there. I survived perfectly. The epic was myself.

An unfamiliar car stopped in front of the building next door.

New people moving in: new foreigners for warehousing in the ghetto so that they would not contaminate the Chinese.

The car contained large suitcases and four people, among them the center of the world.

The center of the world lived 44 yards from me.

The center of the world was an Italian national named Elena.

Elena became the center of the world the moment

her feet touched the concrete pavement of San Li Tun.

Her father was a small nervous Italian. Her mother was from Surinam, a tall Amerindian with eyes that were disconcerting, Shining Path-strange.

Elena was six years old, and as beautiful as an angel in an art book.

She had dark eyes, immense and steady-gazed, and skin the color of sand on a dampened beach.

Her hair, black as Bakelite, shone as if each strand had been waxed individually, and plunged down her back towards her buttocks.

Her lovely nose would have knocked all thought out of Pascal's head.

Her cheeks formed a celestial oval, yet one had only to behold the perfection of her mouth to understand how wicked she was.

Her body epitomized universal harmony, dense and delicate, with a child's smoothness. Her contours were extraordinarily distinct, as if she wished to stand out more clearly that anyone else against the screen of the world.

Compared with a proper description of Elena, the Song of Songs was a shopping list.

With a single look, one knew that Elena was to suffering as Grevisse's *Le Bon Usage* is to French grammar: a classic both unbearable and indispensable.

On that day she wore a frock of white *broderie anglaise*. I would have died of shame if I'd had to wear such a thing. But Elena was far outside our system of values, and in that dress she seemed like an angel in full bloom.

She stepped down from the car without seeing me.

In general terms, that was her policy for the entire year we were to spend together.

China's mythification obeys certain laws.

A small lesson in grammar:

It is correct to say "I learned to read in Bulgaria" or "I met Eulalia in Brazil." But it would be wrong to say "I learned to read in China" or "I met Eulalia in China." Correct form demands "It was in China that I learned to read" and "It was in Peking that I met Eulalia."

There is nothing less innocent than syntax. Clearly, this construction may not be used to introduce a banality.

Thus, one cannot say "It was in 1974 that I wiped my nose" or "It was in Peking that I tied my shoelaces." At least, not without adding "for the first time," since without it the statement sounds awkward.

This has a surprising consequence: if accounts of China always seem extraordinary, it is above all for grammatical reasons.

Analysts of style will find this meeting of syntax and mythology perfectly acceptable. And, their requirements having been satisfied, one can then risk writing the following: "It was in China that I discovered freedom."

That scandalous sentence may be reinterpreted as: "It was in the horrifying China of the Gang of Four that I discovered freedom."

And that absurd sentence may be further reinterpreted as: "It was in the prison-like ghetto of San Li Tun that I discovered freedom."

Such a shocking assertion can be excused only by the fact that it was true.

In that nightmare of a country, the adult foreigners lived depressed and uneasy lives. What they saw revolted them; what they didn't see revolted them even more.

Their children, however, were having the time of their lives.

The sufferings of the Chinese people did not concern them in the least. And being dumped in a concrete ghetto with hundreds of other children was like being on holiday.

For me even more than the others, this was when I discovered freedom. I had just arrived after several years in Japan. I had spent nursery school in the Japanese educational system — that is to say, in the army. In my parents' house, governesses had taken close care of me.

In San Li Tun, no one watched over the children. We were so numerous and the space so limited that it didn't seem necessary. By some sort of unwritten law, parents left their progeny alone from the moment of their arrival in Peking. They went out together in the evening to avoid wallowing in depression and left us to ourselves. With the naiveté typical of their years, they thought we were tired out and in our beds by nine.

In fact, each evening we delegated someone to watch for the adults. News of their return precipitated a general retreat. The children dashed to their respective jails, leapt into bed with their clothes on, and feigned sleep.

For war was most beautiful at night. The enemy's cries of fear echoed better in the darkness, ambushes took on an added mystery, and my role as a pathfinder grew more luminous: on my cantering horse, I felt like a living torch. I was not Prometheus, I was fire itself, exhilarated by the sight of my furtive glimmering against the immense darkness of the Chinese walls.

War was the noblest of games. The word itself resonated like a treasure chest: one forced its lock and riches flashed before our faces: doubloons, pearls and gems, yes, but above all mad violence, sumptuous risks, pillage, terror. And, diamond of diamonds, the license, the freedom that howled about our ears and made us titans.

So we were confined to the ghetto — big deal! Freedom wasn't calculated in square feet. In the end, freedom was to be left to ourselves. Adults can give their children no finer gift than to forget about them.

Forgotten by both the Chinese and parental authorities, the children of San Li Tun were the only autonomous individuals in the entire People's

Republic. Ecstasy, heroism, and divine wickedness were ours.

Playing at anything but war would have been demeaning.

That is what Elena would never understand.

In fact, there was nothing Elena wanted to understand.

From the very first, she acted as if she already understood everything. And she was very convincing. She had her opinions and she never attempted to prove them.

She spoke little, with self-confidence both condescending and offhand.

"I don't want to play war. It isn't interesting."

I was relieved to be the only one to hear such blasphemy, and I resolved to hush up the incident. It was essential that the Allies not think badly of my beloved.

"War is magnificent," I corrected her.

She appeared not to hear. She had a gift for appearing not to hear.

She always appeared to need nothing and no one.

She lived her life as if it were perfectly sufficient to be the most beautiful little girl in the world, and to have such long hair.

I had never had friends, of either gender. I'd never even thought of it. What could they offer me? I was happy with my own company.

I needed parents, enemies, and comrades-in-arms. To a lesser extent, I needed slaves and spectators — *noblesse oblige*. Anyone not belonging to the above categories might as well not have existed, and friends even less so.

My parents had friends. These were people they saw in order to drink alcohol, which came in various colors. As if one couldn't drink on one's own!

Apart from that, the function of friends was to talk and to listen. One told them pointless stories, they laughed loudly and replied with other stories. And then they ate.

Sometimes friends danced. A worrisome spectacle.

In sum, friends were a species of person in whose company one engaged in absurd, even grotesque, activities, or normal activities for which their presence was unnecessary.

To have friends was a symptom of degeneracy.

My brother and sister had friends. This was excusable, however, since these individuals were also their comrades-in-arms. Such friendship, borne in the fraternity of combat, was nothing to blush about.

As for me, I was a pathfinder. Mine was a solitary combat. Friendship was for other people.

As for love, it concerned me even less. It was an abnormality linked to geography: the *Tales of the Arabian Nights* indicated frequent outbreaks of it in the Middle East. I was too far east to be affected.

Contrary to what one might believe, my attitude

towards others had nothing to do with vanity. It was purely logical. All roads led to me: it wasn't my fault, or my decision. It was a given, a fact of life. What did I need friends for? They had no role to play in my existence. I was the center of the world: there was nothing they could do to make me more central.

The only relationship that mattered was with one's horse.

My encounter with Elena was not a transfer of power — I had none and didn't worry about it — but an intellectual shift: henceforth, the center of the world was situated outside of me. And I did everything I could to get closer to it.

I discovered that it was not enough to be close to her. I also had to count for something in her eyes, which was not the case. I didn't interest her. In truth, nothing seemed to interest her. She looked at nothing and said nothing. She seemed content within herself. All the same, one sensed that she felt one's eyes on her, and that it pleased her.

It took me some time to understand that only one thing counted for Elena: to be gazed at.

Without knowing it, I made her happy: I devoured her with my gaze. It was impossible to take my eyes off her. I'd never seen anything so beautiful. It was the first time that someone's beauty had struck me. I had already met many good-looking people but they hadn't held my attention. For reasons that I still don't understand, Elena's beauty obsessed me.

I loved her from the first second I saw her. How does one explain such things? I'd never thought of loving anyone, never dreamed that someone's beauty could awaken any feelings in me. And yet everything was set in motion at that first moment, with an inexorable authority: she was the fairest, therefore I loved her, therefore she became the center of the world.

The mystery deepened. I understood that it was not enough to love her: she must also love me. Why? That's the way it was.

I let her know this in all simplicity. It was natural that I inform her:

"You have to love me."

She deigned to look at me, but it was not the look I wanted. She gave a disdainful little laugh. It was clear that I had just said something idiotic. So I had to explain to her why it wasn't.

"You have to love me because I love you. You understand?"

I thought that this additional information put everything back into order. Yet Elena's laughter increased.

I began to feel pain and confusion.

"Why are you laughing?"

Her voice was amused, haughty, and matter-of-fact:

"Because you're dumb."

And that was how my first declaration of love was received.

♦

In one go, I was discovering awe, love, altruism, and humiliation. This hand was dealt me, in that order, on the first day. I concluded that there must be logical links between the four phenomena. It would therefore have been better to avoid the first, but it was too late. In any case, I wasn't sure that I'd had any choice in the matter.

And I found the situation most regrettable. Because it also acquainted me with suffering. An extraordinarily unpleasant feeling.

Nonetheless, suffering never brought me to regret my love for Elena, or to regret her existence. One couldn't be unhappy that one such as she existed. And if she existed, it was inevitable to love her.

From the first second that I'd loved her — the very first second — I realized I had to do something. This leitmotif took hold by itself and never released me until that love ended.

"I must do something."

"Because I love Elena, because she is the fairest, because such a celestial creature walks the earth, because I've met her, because — even if she doesn't know it — she is my love, I must do something."

"Something grand, something superb — something worthy of her and my love."

"Kill a German, for instance. But they'd never let me do that. We always finish by releasing them alive.

The adults and the Geneva Convention strike again. This war is rigged."

"No. It has to be something I do on my own. Something that will impress Elena."

I felt a wave of despair, which cut my legs out from under me. I sank down on the concrete. My feeling of powerlessness rendered me incapable of the slightest movement.

I wanted never to move again. I wanted to waste away. I would remain there, seated on the concrete, doing nothing, drinking nothing, eating nothing, until I died. Then I would die very quickly and my beloved would be very moved.

No, that wouldn't work. They would come and force-feed me through a funnel. The adults would make me ridiculous.

So it had to be the opposite. Since sitting still was not an option, I would move. And then we'd see what we would see. Some prodigious effort, something to shift this body that suffering had turned to stone.

I ran to the stables and mounted my steed with a single bound.

The sentinels let me pass without any problem.

(The perfunctory performance of the Chinese guards always astonished me. I was a little offended that they didn't find me more suspicious. During my three years in San Li Tun, they never searched me. There was something rotten in this system.)

On the Boulevard of Habitable Ugliness, I

launched my horse into the most vertiginous gallop in the history of motion.

Nothing could stop me. I could not say whether horse or rider was more intoxicated. Propelled by rocket fuel, my brain soon went supersonic. A porthole in the fuselage exploded into fragments, and my mind was sucked outside in an instant. A shrieking void filled my head, and both suffering and thought were left far behind.

My horse and I were an unguided missile in the City of Electric Fans.

At that time, there were few cars in Peking. One could gallop without stopping at street corners, without looking, without paying attention.

My crazy ride lasted for four hours.

When I returned to the ghetto, all that remained of me was a blur of confusion.

"I must do something." Well, I had done something. I had lost myself in motion for hours across the city.

Of course, Elena knew nothing about it, and in a certain way that made it even better. Such selfless nobility filled me with pride. But not to tell Elena about it would have been a waste.

The next day, I approached her with a knowing look.

She did not deign to look at me.

I wasn't worried. She would see me.

I sat down next to her on the wall and said nonchalantly, "I've got a horse."

She looked at me incredulously. I thrilled to it.

"A toy horse?"

"A horse I gallop all over the place."

"A horse here in San Li Tun? Where is it?"

Her curiosity enchanted me. I ran to the stables and returned on horseback.

One look was enough for my beloved. She shrugged and said with utter indifference, without even the charity of sarcasm, "That's not a horse, that's a bicycle."

"It's a horse," I assured her calmly.

My unruffled conviction did no good. Elena wasn't listening any more.

In Peking, owning a bike was as normal as owning a pair of legs. My bicycle had taken such a mythic dimension in my life that it had achieved equine status. This status was so established in my eyes that it took no leap of faith to show the animal to people. It hadn't occurred to me that Elena might see in it something other than a horse.

To this day, it is something I still find mysterious. I wasn't playing out some childish fantasy, I hadn't concocted some fairy-tale substitution. The bike was a horse, and that is how it was. I don't remember a particular moment in which I decided anything about it. The horse had always been a horse. It could not be otherwise. That animal of flesh and blood was as much a

43

part of objective reality as the giant fans I'd sneered at during my gallops around the city. In all sincerity, I believed that the center of the world would see things as I did.

I hadn't even gotten to the second day and already this love was putting my mental universe in peril.

The Copernican revolution was a joke in comparison. My only hope was obstinacy. My article of faith was contained in a single sentence: "Elena is blind."

The only way to stop suffering was to clear my mind of all but emptiness. And the only way to completely empty my mind was to move as fast as possible, to launch my horse into a gallop, muzzle to the wind, to become an extension of my charging mount, the horn of the unicorn, with no mission but to cleave the air — unto the final joust, in which rider and mount, lost in their headlong rush and sucked up and pulverized by Peking's giant fans, would disintegrate and be absorbed by the ether.

Elena is blind. This horse is a horse. A horse born of motion and the wind, liberty made manifest. To me, a horse is not the thing that has four legs and produces manure, but the force that defies the earth and carries me away from it, hoists me up and keeps me aloft, would trample me to death if I surrendered to the mud's siren call, makes my heart dance and my guts whinny, which whirls me into motion so frenetic that I must close my eyelids tight, for not even the purest light dazzles so much as the wind's blast.

A horse is that unique place where it is possible to lose all anchorage, all thought, all consciousness, all idea of tomorrow, where one is nothing more than an upward leap and a headlong charge.

A horse is access to the infinite, and riding is that moment of unity with the Mongols, the Tartars, the Saracens, the Sioux, and other mounted comrades who have lived to ride, to *be*.

Riding is the spirit that leaps from four hooves, and I know that my bicycle has four hooves and that it leaps and that it is a horse.

A rider is she whose horse has torn her from stagnation, and restored her to the whistling rush of freedom.

For all these reasons, never has a horse so deserved the name as mine.

If Elena were not blind, she would see that the bicycle was a horse and she would love me.

It was only the second day, and already I had lost face twice.

For the Chinese, losing face was the worst thing that could happen.

I wasn't Chinese, but I agreed with the concept. That double humiliation profoundly dishonored me. Some striking deed was needed to regain my honor. Anything less and Elena would not love me.

I awaited the moment uneasily.

I dreaded the third day.

Each time we tortured one of the German kids, the opposing camp would beat up one of our number in reprisal. Which led to revenge, and so on. From one punitive expedition to the next, the belligerent forces could justify all of their crimes.

This is what one calls war.

People make fun of children who justify dirty deeds with a whining "He started it!" Yet no adult conflict is born otherwise.

In San Li Tun, it was the Allies who started it. But one of the vices of History is that one can find the beginnings wherever one wishes.

The East Germans never failed to cite our first attack in the heart of the ghetto. We found this geographic limitation petty. The war hadn't begun in 1972 in Peking. Its origin was European and went back to 1939.

A few budding intellectuals brought up the armistice of 1945. We jeered at their naivety. What happened in 1945 was the same as had happened in 1918: the soldiers had called time-out to catch their breath.

We had caught our breath and the enemy had not changed.

Not a bad base to build on.

◆

One of the most terrible episodes of the war was the battle of the hospital and its consequences.

Among the military secrets that each of the Allies had to keep quiet was the hospital. We had left the famous moving crate where it was. From the outside, our installation was invisible.

The rule was that one had to enter the hospital as discreetly as possible, and always one at a time. No problem: the crate sat alongside the brickworks wall. Sneaking in there was — so to speak — child's play.

As well, these Germans were the world's most inept spies. They had never pinpointed any of our bases. War with them was too easy.

Barring informers, we had nothing to worry about. And it was impossible that there might be traitors among us. Our ranks included a few cowards, but no criminals.

Falling into enemy hands meant getting beaten up: it was a nasty thing to happen, but we all stood up to it. We never felt that this form of abuse really constituted torture. It never entered our minds that one of us would betray a military secret to escape so insignificant a punishment.

And yet, that is what happened.

Elena had a ten-year-old brother. To the same degree that Elena stood out because of her beauty and detachment, Claudio was stunningly ridiculous. Not that he was ugly or malformed, but even his smallest gestures betrayed a limp affectedness, a mediocrity, and a lack of confidence that grated from the moment one laid eyes on him. As well, like his sister, he was always dressed in his Sunday best. The part in his glowingly clean hair was always straight, and his perfectly ironed clothes seemed taken from some fashion catalogue for the children of apparatchiks.

All of this gave us excellent reason to hate him.

We could not, however, refuse to let him join our ranks. Elena thought the war ridiculous and looked down on us. Claudio, on the other hand, saw it as a means of social integration and thoroughly abased himself in order to be admitted.

And so he was. We could not risk offending our numerous Italian soldiers — who included the irreplaceable Jihan — by rejecting one of their compatriots. What was even more irritating was the fact that they themselves detested the newcomer. But then, their sensitivities overflowed with disconcerting paradoxes.

No big deal. Claudio would be a lousy soldier, nothing more. The army couldn't count on everyone being a hero.

Two weeks after he joined up, in the course of a mêlée, Elena's brother was captured by the Germans. We had never seen anyone defend himself so badly or run so slowly.

In our hearts, we were happy. The idea of the punches he was going to receive filled us with joy. Our sympathies were with the enemy, especially since the Italian boy was so scared of pain and his mother babied him so much it was sickening.

Claudio returned limping, but with no trace of bumps or bruises. Snivelling, he told us that the Germans had twisted his foot a full 360 degrees. We were amazed to hear of these new tactics.

On the following day, a Teutonic offensive reduced the hospital to kindling, and Elena's brother forgot to limp. We understood. Claudio didn't speak much English, but enough to betray us.

(English was our language of communication with the enemy. However, since our exchanges were limited to blows and torture, we had little occasion to use it. All of the Allies spoke French, a phenomenon that seemed only natural to me.)

The Italian soldiers were the first to demand punishment for the informer. It was during our council of war that Claudio revealed the full profundity of his cowardice: his mother arrived in person, ordering us to spare the boy.

"If you touch a hair of my son's head, I'll give you a thrashing you'll never forget," she said with a fearsome look.

The accused was pardoned but became a living symbol of shame. Our contempt for him knew no bounds.

Any means would serve to get me closer to Elena. She had certainly got wind of the affair from her mother and brother. I told her my version of the story.

Her haughty air could not hide a certain pain. I understood: if André or Juliette had proven guilty of such an felony, their dishonor would have stained me too.

In any case, that was how I approached the subject with Elena. I wanted to be the one who saw her vulnerability. Surely such a sublime creature could have no other weak point than her brother.

It was clear to me that she wouldn't admit defeat.

"Anyway, war is ridiculous," she said with her usual disdain.

"Ridiculous or not, Claudio cried until we let him fight the war with us."

She knew that my argument was irrefutable. She made no reply, and retreated into the self-sufficiency of her silence.

And yet, for a moment I had seen her suffer. For the space of a second, she had been within reach.

I felt it as an overwhelming victory of love.

At dawn, in my bed, I reran the scene.

It truly seemed to me that I had touched the sublime.

Is there, in the heart of some great culture, a mythological episode of this type? "The spurned lover, in hopes of moving his unreachable beloved, informs her that her brother is a traitor."

To my knowledge, such a scene has never been

played out in its full pathos. The great classics would never have admitted conduct so base.

The vile side of this escaped me entirely. And even if I had been aware of it, I doubt it would have bothered me: this love so possessed me that I would not have hesitated to cover myself with ignominy. For how important was my honor now? It wasn't important, since I was nothing. So long as I had been the center of the world, I'd had a rank to maintain. Now, it was Elena's rank that mattered.

I blessed Claudio's existence. Without him, there would have been no breach, no access, if not to the heart of my beloved, then at least to her honor.

I reran the scene: me, before her customary indifference. She: beautiful, purely beautiful, not deigning to be anything else but beautiful.

And then the shameful words: your brother, my beloved, your brother whom you do not love — for you love no one but yourself — but nonetheless your brother, inseparable from your honor, your brother, my divine one, is a coward and a criminal of the worst order.

This fleeting, sublime moment in which I had seen that, because of my news, something in you, something indefinable — and therefore important — was laid bare! By me!

My goal was not to make you suffer. In fact, the goal of this love was not known to me. All I knew was that in the service of my passion, I needed to provoke in you a real emotion, any emotion.

That tiny hint of pain behind your eyes, what supreme reward for my efforts!

I re-ran the scene, freeze-framing as I went. I surrendered to an adoring trance. From now on I would be a someone for Elena.

It couldn't stop there. She had to suffer some more. I was too craven to do the hurting myself, but I resolved to find whatever information might wound her, and to always be the one who brought her the bad news.

I was even beginning to have strange dreams. Elena's mother killing herself in a traffic accident. The Italian ambassador firing her father. Claudio walking about with a hole in the seat of his pants, the laughingstock of the entire ghetto.

All of these catastrophes obeyed the same rule: they never hurt Elena herself, only those who mattered to her.

These fantasies delighted me to the depths of my soul. I pictured myself walking up to my beloved, my face terribly solemn, and saying in slow, grave tones: "Elena, your mother is dead," or "Your brother has dishonored himself."

Pain lashes your face: the sight of this strikes my heart and I love you all the more.

Yes, my beloved, you suffer because of me. Not that I love suffering; it would be better if I could bring you happiness, but I understand that isn't possible; for me to bring you happiness it would first be necessary for you to love me, and you don't love me, whereas it isn't necessary that you love me for me to bring you pain, and anyway, to make you happy it would first be necessary for you to be unhappy — how can one make someone happy if she is already happy — and therefore I must first make you unhappy in order to have a chance at then making you happy, and in any case it only counts if it is because of me, my beloved. If you could feel for me even one-tenth of what I feel for you, you would be glad to suffer, knowing the pleasure you bring me in doing so.

I swooned with sheer pleasure.

We needed a new hospital.

It was not a question of simply setting up in another moving crate. Our choices were very limited. It was inevitable that we would end up administering medical services in the same place where we prepared and kept the Secret Weapon. It was far from hygienic, but China had accustomed us to dirt.

New beds of *The People's Daily* were duly constructed at the top of the fire escape of San Li Tun's highest building. The Secret Weapon commanded the center of this high-altitude dormitory.

The Germans had been stupid enough to spare our reserves of sterile gauze, vitamin C, and soup packets. We put them in knapsacks and suspended them from the balustrades of the metal staircase. Since it almost never rained in Peking, our reserves were in no danger from the elements. But our secret base became much more visible. All the Germans had to do was point their noses upwards and look attentively, and they'd have seen us. We were never so stupid as to take a prisoner up there; when we wanted to torture a victim, we brought the Secret Weapon down.

The war now took on an unexpected political dimension.

One morning we tried to walk up to our headquarters. To our amazement: the door to the fire escape had been padlocked.

And it wasn't difficult to determine that the lock was not German. It was Chinese.

So, the ghetto guards had discovered our headquarters. It had so enraged them that they had taken the monstrous measure of locking up an emergency fire escape — the only fire escape in San Li Tun's tallest building. In case of fire, the inhabitants could have escaped only by throwing themselves out of the windows.

This scandalous event delighted us.

With reason. Is it not wonderful to discover that you have a new enemy?

And what an enemy: China itself! Living in this country had already ennobled us. Fighting it gave us truly heroic status.

One day we would be able to tell our descendants, voices resonant with grandeur, that we had made war, in Peking, against the Germans and against the Chinese. The height of glory.

And even more, the wonderful news: our enemy

was an idiot. He constructed fire escapes and then locked them up. This logical inconsistency delighted us. It was as stupid as building a swimming pool and then not putting a drop of water in it.

We actually longed for this fire to occur. After an inquest, it would be revealed to the world that the Chinese people had in effect condemned hundreds of foreigners to death. As well as being heroes, we would gain the status of the politically oppressed — international martyrs. Truly, our time in this country would not have been wasted.

(Actually, we were totally naive. Had there been such a fire and a subsequent inquest, the scandal of the lock would have been carefully hushed up.)

Obviously, we hid this juicy information from our parents. Their intervention would have ruined our chances of martyrdom. Besides, we hated it when the adults stuck their noses in our affairs. They sucked the flavor out of everything. They were entirely without a sense of the epic. All they ever thought about was human rights, tennis, and bridge. They seemed to have no idea that for once in their insignificant lives, the opportunity was theirs to become heroes.

Such banality: they held fast to life and existence. So did we, in fact, but only under conditions that ennoble that existence — for example, by sacrificing it to a nice big fire.

(The truth was, if such a fire had broken out, we would have borne some of the responsibility in the same way as the Chinese guards. We were vaguely aware of this, but not at all bothered by it. For myself, I cared even less since neither Elena nor my family lived in that building.)

The excellent news had one significant drawback, however, that could not be ignored: we no longer had access to our headquarters.

Yet the very statement of the problem provided its solution: the padlock was Chinese. A metal nail file was enough to crack it. And to keep the guards from figuring it out, we had the presence of mind to buy an identical padlock, to which we had the key, and put it in the old one's place.

If there had been a fire, we would have been the main culprits; it would have been our padlock that condemned the victims to death.

We were vaguely aware of this as well. But it wasn't a problem. After all, this was Peking, not Geneva. We'd never had the slightest intention of waging a clean war.

We didn't particularly desire loss of life. But if death were necessary for the war to continue, then there would be death.

In any case, such side issues didn't concern us greatly.

De minimis non curat praetor. It was normal for adults, those children fallen from grace, to waste time over such questions. They never knew what to do with their time anyway.

We, on the other hand, had such an acute sense of human values that we rarely mentioned people over the age of fifteen. They belonged to a parallel world, one with which we had good relations because our paths hardly crossed at all.

Nor did we spend much time on the stupid question of our future. Possibly because we instinctively had already discovered the only real response: "When I'm grown up, I'll think about when I was a kid."

Clearly, adulthood was devoted to childhood. Parents and their accomplices existed only so that their offspring wouldn't have to worry about ancillary questions such as food and board. In other words, so that they could devote themselves entirely to their essential role — that of being children, i.e., *being*.

Kids who can speak at length about their future have always intrigued me. When anyone asked me that stock question "What will you be when you grow up?" I invariably replied that I would either be a Nobel Prize winner or a martyr, or perhaps both. I always said this quickly, and not in order to make an impression: on the contrary, this pre-packaged answer allowed me to escape as quickly as possible from the absurd subject.

More abstract than absurd: in my heart, I believed that I would never become an adult. Time took far too long for that moment ever to arrive. I was seven years old: these eighty-four months had seemed interminable. My life was taking forever! The very idea that

I might live through an equal number of months made me dizzy. Seven more years. No. Impossible. Surely I would stop at ten or eleven, saturated. I already felt near saturation as it was: so much had happened to me.

Whenever I mentioned my martyrdom or my Nobel Prize in medicine, it wasn't from vanity: it was an abstract response to an abstract question. In any case, I didn't see anything so awe-inspiring in either occupation. The only profession for which I had real respect was soldiering, and in particular the rank of pathfinder. I was already at the summit of my career. Afterwards — if there were an afterwards — would come the fall, and I would have to content myself with the Nobel. But I never seriously believed such an afterwards would come to pass.

This skepticism was accompanied by another: when adults talked about their childhood, it always struck me that they were lying. They had never been children. They had been adults for all eternity. The fall was a myth, for children stayed children just as adults stayed adults.

I kept this unformulated conviction to myself. I understood that I could never defend it: for that reason I believed it all the more strongly.

Elena never told anyone that that my bicycle was a horse, or vice versa.

It wasn't a sign of any particular goodness on her

part: it was because I was of no importance. She never spoke about non-entities.

In fact, she spoke very little. And she never spoke up first: she was content to answer questions that didn't seem beneath her.

"What will you be when you grow up?" I asked her one day, purely out of scientific interest.

No answer.

Looking back, her attitude confirms my views. Children who answer such a question quickly are either pseudo-children (there are many such) or children with a taste for abstraction and pure speculation (which was my case).

Elena was a true child, with no bent for speculative thought. Answering such a question would have meant lowering herself. One might as well have asked a tightrope walker what she would do if she were an accountant.

"Where'd you get your dress?"

That was something she would answer. Usually with, "Mama made it. She sews extremely well."

Or sometimes: "Mama bought it for me in Turin."

That was the city she came from. To me, Baghdad seemed no more exotic.

She almost always wore white. The color suited her perfectly.

Her glossy hair was so long that even in braids it still went down to her bottom. Her mother would never have authorized a Chinese to touch it: only she could braid her daughter's glory, which she did slow-ly and passionately.

I preferred to have a single braid, but Trê most often made me two, as she wore them herself. On those days that I got a single braid, I felt very elegant. In fact, I had the greatest respect for my hair until the day I discovered Elena's: from then on, mine seemed trivial. This truth appeared to me on the day that, by coinci-dence, our hair had been made up in the same way. My braid was long and dark; hers was endless and sparkled jet black.

Elena was a year younger than me and I was a good two inches taller, yet she was my superior in everything. She surpassed me as she surpassed the entire world. She had so little need of other people that she seemed older than me.

She was able to spend entire days pacing the ghet-to in small, unhurried steps. She looked about her just enough to see that she was being looked at.

I ask myself if there were any children who didn't watch her. She inspired admiration, respect, delight, and fear — because she was the fairest and because she was always serene, because she never made the first moves in human contact, because you had to come to her in order to enter her world, and because the truth was that no one entered her world, which must have been one of extraordinary luxury, extraordinary calm, and extraordinary pleasure, wherein she could glory in her perfection.

♦

No one watched her as much as I did.

Since 1974, there have been many whom I have gazed at long and avidly — to the point of making them uncomfortable.

But Elena was the first.

And it didn't bother her in the least.

It was she who taught me to watch people. Because she was beautiful, because she seemed to demand close watching. A demand I satisfied with rare zeal.

Because of her, my military effectiveness began to decline. The pathfinder found less. Before Elena, I spent most of my free time in the saddle, scouting the enemy. Now it was necessary to devote numerous hours to watching Elena. This could be done on foot or on horseback, but always from a respectful distance.

It never occurred to me how inept I might have appeared. When I looked at her, I forgot I existed. My forgetfulness led to all sorts of weird behavior.

It was at night, in bed, that I remembered my existence. And then I suffered; I loved Elena and I felt in my bones that this love called up something. I had no idea of the nature of this something. I knew that, at the very least, she should care about me: that was the first stage, and an indispensable one. But after that, I felt, there had to be some obscure and indefinable exchange. I invented stories for myself — which some might call metaphors — in order to approach this mystery. In these experimental tales, the love-object was always terribly cold. Most often, she appeared covered in snow. Scantily dressed, and often nude, she wept with the cold. Snow played a considerable role.

I liked the fact that she was so cold, because it meant that she would have to be warmed up. My imagination wasn't sufficiently acute to find the ideal method for doing so; on the other hand, I revelled in thinking about — or feeling — the heat that slowly and exquisitely invaded her ice-bound body, that soothed her frostbite and made her breathe with a singular pleasure.

These stories lifted me to states of mind so beautiful that I thought them supernatural. The power of their magic reflected itself on me: it conferred upon me the status of medium. I wielded prodigious secrets, and if only Elena were aware of this, she would love me.

It still remained for her to be made aware.

I set myself to this task. My tactic, one of astonishing naivety, proves to what point I believed in this ineffable magic.

One morning, I approached her. She was wearing a sleeveless purple dress, which fit snugly to her waist then flowered out like a peony. Her graceful beauty filled my head with fog.

I remembered, however, what I had to say to her.

"Elena, I have a secret."

She deigned to look at me, her demeanor allowing that stray facts were always worth a listen.

"Another horse?" she asked with restrained irony.

"No. A real secret. Something no one else on earth knows."

I had no doubt whatsoever of this.

"What is it?"

I then realized — and at that point it was a bit late — that I was absolutely unable to express it. What could I say to her? I couldn't exactly tell her about the snow and her strange sighs.

It was horrible. The first time I had her full attention, and I had nothing to say.

I escaped using a delaying tactic:

"Follow me."

And I began to walk in no particular direction, but with a determined air to hide my panicked confusion.

Miraculously, she followed me. Not that this was such an extraordinary concession for her: she spent her days walking slowly around the ghetto. Today she was content to do so in my company, by my side but as distant as always.

It was hard to walk at such a relaxed pace. I felt like I was shooting a film in slow motion. And this unease was paltry compared with my inner terror that I had nothing — nothing! — to show her.

At the same time, it gave me a triumphant feeling to see her walking at my side. I had never seen her walking with anyone. Her hair was pulled back in a braid, so that her lovely profile was revealed to me in all its distinct clarity.

But where in heaven's name could I take her? The ghetto held no secrets, and she knew this as well as I did.

The episode must have lasted a good half hour. In my memory it lasts a week. Me, walking incredibly slowly, as much to keep in step with Elena as to stave off my inevitable humiliation — that moment of shame when I would show her some hole in the pavement or a broken brick, or some other idiocy, and when I would dare to pronounce some enormity like, "Oh! Someone stole it. Who could have taken my box of emeralds?" My beloved would laugh in my face. The jaws of defeat yawned all around me.

I had exposed myself to ridicule and yet I could not fault myself, for I knew that the secret did indeed exist and that it was far more than some box of emeralds. If only I could have found the words to describe to Elena the mystery's sublime beauty — the snow, the bizarre warmth, the unknown pleasures, the wonderful smiles, and the even less explicable events to follow.

If I could have shown her even a glimpse of these wonders, she would have admired me, and then loved me — I was sure of it. Words cut me off from her. If only I could find the right formula to open the treasure, like Ali Baba's "Open, sesame!" But the great mystery hid its language from me, and all I could do was walk ever more slowly, vaguely hoping for the miraculous apparition of something — an elephant, a winged boat, a nuclear reactor — that would provide a diversion.

Elena's patience attested to her lack of curiosity, as if she had decided in advance that my secret would be disappointing. I almost thanked her for it. Pace by unhurried pace, pointless hither by idiotic yon, my itinerary took us to the gates of the ghetto.

A jolt of despair and anger shook me. I was on the verge of throwing myself on the ground and shrieking:

"The secret is no place I can show you! I can't even explain it. But it's real! You've got to believe me — I feel it inside myself, and it's a zillion times more beautiful than anything you can imagine! And you've got to love me, I'm the only person who possesses it. Don't pass up something as extraordinary as me!"

It was at that moment that Elena unwittingly saved me:

"Is your secret outside of San Li Tun?"

I said yes only for something to say, knowing perfectly well that the Boulevard of Habitable Ugliness hid nothing that might even vaguely pass for a secret.

My beloved stopped in her tracks.

"Oh, well then. I'm not allowed to leave San Li Tun."

"You're not?" I asked, straight-faced, scarcely believing this last-minute reprieve.

"Mama says I can't. She says the Chinese are dangerous."

I almost shouted, *"Vive le racisme!"* but contented myself with the appropriate tag to the episode:

"That's too bad! If you could only see how fabulous it is!"

As the poet Mallarmé himself said on his deathbed.

Elena shrugged and wandered off.

I must confess: since that day, I have retained a deep and abiding appreciation for Chinese communism.

Two horses passed through the ghetto's only gate, which was always guarded. On reaching the Boulevard of Habitable Ugliness, they rode left rather than turn towards the Square of the Great Fan. They were leaving the city.

The Square of the Great Fan was the location of the Forbidden City. In truth, it was less forbidden than the countryside. But the two knights were too young for restrictions, and no one stopped them.

As they galloped along the road to the country, the City of Electric Fans faded behind them.

One cannot fully understand how sad the world can be without having seen the farmlands that surround Peking. It is difficult to imagine the grandest empire in history rising from something so poor.

A desert is a thing of beauty. But a desert disguised as farmland is a sorry spectacle. The fields looked exhausted. The few human beings were invisible, for their hovels were holes dug into the earth.

If any countryside on this planet can be described as desolate, this is the one. The hooves of the two horses hammered the narrow road, as if trying to drown out the sepulchral silence.

I am not sure whether my sister knew that her bicycle was a horse. In any case, nothing in her demeanor contradicted this mythical truth.

We finally arrived at a pond surrounded by rice paddies. After dismounting and taking off our armor, we plunged into the muddy water. This was our Saturday expedition.

From time to time a Chinese peasant, his face prodigiously empty, approached to view the two white objects afloat in the pond.

The two knights climbed out of the water, redonned their armor, and sat down on the ground. While their chargers foraged among the scrabbly grass, they ate tea biscuits.

School began in September.

For me, it was nothing new. But it was Elena's first time.

In actual fact, Peking's little French school had little to do with education. We, the children of all nations — English- and German-speakers excepted — would have been astonished to be told we attended that establishment in order to learn. It never occurred to us.

For me, the school was a factory dedicated to the production of paper airplanes. Even the professors lent a hand in making them. This should not be too surprising: since none of them were qualified teachers, it was about all they were capable of doing.

Volunteers all, these worthy individuals had ended up in China by accident — for one may properly term an accident the sum of such massive initial illusions and such crushing subsequent disappointments.

Apart from the diplomats and sinologists, all of the foreigners residing in China at that time were there for the same "accidental" reasons. And since these lost souls had to occupy themselves somehow, they ended up "teaching" at Peking's little French school.

It was my first school. The place where I spent the three years reputed to be the most important in one's life. Yet, try as I might to jog my memory, I can't remember learning anything there beyond the construction of paper airplanes.

It didn't matter particularly. I had been reading since I was four, writing since I was five, and tying my own shoelaces since prehistoric times. I had, therefore, nothing left to learn.

The teachers were faced with a superhuman task: preventing the children from killing each other. And they succeeded. These admirable individuals are therefore to be congratulated, and it behooves one to understand that, under such conditions, only a nine-teenth century idealist would have attempted extraordinary luxuries such as teaching the alphabet.

We children of many nations understood school to be nothing more than the continuation of war by identical means. With this singular difference: there were no Germans in Peking's little French school. They all went to the East German school.

We resolved this vexatious problem with an arrangement that combined both inspiration and madness: at school, everyone was the enemy.

The establishment's restricted dimensions lent themselves perfectly to our attacking each other. There was no need to seek out the enemy. He was everywhere, near to hand, near to tooth, to foot, to urine, and to vomit; to spit at, to scratch, to butt, and to trip. One had only to choose.

The school's picturesque quality was enhanced by the fact that fully one-quarter of the students spoke no French and had no intention of learning any. Their parents had parked them there because they truly had no idea what else to do with their children. And because they wanted the peace to savor, in the company of other adults, the joys of the regime in power.

That is why the school included Peruvian kids and other extraterrestrials, whom we tortured at will and whose terrified shrieks were absolutely incomprehensible to us. I have the fondest memories of that French school.

◆

It was Elena's first school too.

The idea scared me. I adored that place of perdition, but the idea of a creature like her in such a jungle was terrifying. She who so hated physical violence!

I vowed to myself that anyone who touched even a hair of her head would immediately get my fist in his face. It would give me a chance to look good in her eyes, especially since all the likely aggressors were tougher than I was and would beat me to a pulp — thus making me irresistible in the eyes of the intended victim.

It wasn't necessary.

A miracle occurred wherever Elena went. From the first day of school, a bubble of peace, gentleness, and courtesy formed itself around my beloved. She could traverse the bloodiest of battles, and the bubble would accompany her every step. The reaction was universal, natural and instinctive: no one would attack something so beautiful and so dignified.

At four o'clock she returned to the ghetto as clean and tidy as she'd been in the morning.

The insurrectional atmosphere of the school didn't seem to bother her; she didn't even notice it. During our recreation periods she walked the dusty little schoolyard at her usual unhurried pace, thoughts elsewhere, happy in her solitude.

The inevitable occurred: that solitude came to an end.

A beauty as superior as hers imposed a respectful distance. I never imagined another person might be so bold as to dare approach her. My love had introduced me to various forms of suffering, but jealousy had not been one of them.

Imagine my shock, one morning in the schoolyard, when I beheld a fresh-faced boy talking a mile a minute to the Italian girl.

And she, actually standing still to listen to him.

And actually listening. Her head raised towards his. Her eyes and mouth, those of someone listening.

Granted, her manner betrayed no enthusiasm or admiration. But there was no doubt she was listening. She had deigned to pay attention to someone.

Before my eyes, that boy was beginning to exist for her.

And he continued to exist for as many as ten minutes.

And since he was in her class, God only knew how much longer he would exist without me knowing.

The unspeakable infamy of it all.

Some ontological clarifications are required at this point.

Until I was fourteen, I divided humanity into three categories: women, little girls, and buffoons.

All other divisions seemed purely anecdotal: rich or poor, Chinese or Brazilian (Germans were a special case, of course), master or slave, ugly or fair, adult or ancient — these distinctions were obviously important but did not affect an individual's essential nature.

Women were indispensable. They prepared food, dressed their children, taught them to tie their shoelaces; they cleaned things, they manufactured babies in their tummies, they wore interesting clothes.

The buffoons served no purpose at all. Each morning, the grownup buffoons went to the "office," a sort of school for adults, which is to say somewhere pointless. At night they saw their friends — a low activity I've already described.

In fact, big buffoons were little different from small buffoons, leaving aside the not unimportant difference that they had lost the precious gift of childhood. But their functions, like their shapes, hardly changed at all.

In contrast, there was an immense difference between women and little girls. First, they were not of the same gender — one could see this at a single glance. As well, their roles changed enormously with age: they left behind the non-usefulness of childhood for the primordial usefulness of womanhood, whereas the buffoons remained useless all their lives.

The only adult buffoons who did anything worthwhile were the ones who imitated women: cooks, sales clerks, teachers, doctors, and laborers.

These occupations were essentially female, especially the last. On the innumerable propaganda posters found throughout the City of Electric Fans, the workers were all females, round-cheeked and jolly-looking. They repaired electric pylons with such joy that their faces took on a pinkish hue.

The countryside confirmed the reality of the city: the billboards showed nothing but stalwart, cheerful women farmers harvesting sheaves of wheat with evident ecstasy.

The adult buffoons were generally employed in pretend-occupations. For instance, the Chinese soldiers who surrounded the ghetto pretended to be dangerous, but never shot a soul.

I felt a measure of sympathy for the buffoons, mostly because I found their lot a tragic one: they were, after all, born buffoons. They were born with that grotesque thing between their legs that filled them with such pride, and that made them even more buffoonish.

Little buffoons frequently showed me the object, which had the unfailing effect of making me laugh till I was on the verge of tears. This reaction always puzzled them.

One day I was unable to stop myself from saying to one of them, with gentle sincerity:

"Poor thing!"

"Why," he asked, flabbergasted.

"It must be uncomfortable."

"No," he assured me.

"But it must be. What if someone hits you there?"

"That's true. But it's very practical."

"Oh?"

"We can pee standing up."

"So?"

"It's better."

"You think so?"

"Listen, if you want to piss in the Germans' yogurt, you've got to be a boy."

This argument gave me pause. I had no doubt there was a response to this, but what could it be? I would have to puzzle it out later.

Humanity's elite were little girls. Humanity existed so that they could exist.

Women and buffoons were crippled. Their bodies contained errors of construction that could inspire no other reaction but laughter.

Only little girls were perfect. Nothing stuck out from their bodies, no grotesque appendages, no idiotic protuberances. They were of marvellous design, streamlined to present no resistance to life.

Of no material utility, they were the most necessary of all because they embodied humanity's beauty — its real beauty, that which makes living a summer breeze, where nothing clashes and the body is pure celebration from head to foot. One has to have been a little girl to know how exquisite it is to have a body.

What should a body be? An object of pure pleasure and pure festivity.

From the moment one's body begins to display something embarrassing — the moment the body becomes cumbersome — it's all over.

I realize at that moment that the adjective "sleek"

is *non pareil*, which is no surprise: the vocabulary of happiness and pleasure has always been the most impoverished, as it is in all languages.

Therefore allow me to use the word "sleekness" to give an idea, to all those for whom the body has become an encumbrance, of what may be a joyous body.

Plato described the body as a screen, a prison, and I fully agree with him, except in the case of little girls. If Plato had ever been a little girl, he would have known that the body can be exactly the opposite: instrument of all the liberties, springboard to the most delicious dizziness, hopscotch of the soul, jewellery box of virtuosity and speed, the poor mind's only connection to the world. But Plato never even mentions little girls, disregarding them in his Ideal City.

Of course, not all little girls are pretty. But even ugly little girls are a pleasure to see.

And when a little girl is pretty, when a little girl is beautiful, Italy's greatest poet devotes his entire output to her, a towering English logician loses his reason to her, a Russian writer flees his homeland in order to name a dangerous novel after her, and so it goes. Because little girls drive one mad.

Until I was fourteen I liked women and I liked buffoons, but I thought that love for anything but a little girl made no sense at all.

◆

So. When I saw Elena paying attention to a buffoon, I was scandalized.

I could accept that she didn't love me. But that she would prefer a buffoon broke the bounds of absurdity.

Was she blind?

She had a brother; she couldn't be ignorant of boys' disability. Surely she couldn't fall in love with a cripple.

Loving a cripple could only be an act of pity. And pity was foreign to Elena's nature.

It made no sense to me.

Could she really love him? Impossible to know. But she deigned to interrupt her absent strolling for him. She deigned to stop and listen to him. I had never seen her pay so much attention to anyone.

The phenomenon repeated itself during many recreation periods. It was intolerable.

Who the devil was this young buffoon? I didn't know him.

I made inquiries. He was French, six years old, and lived in Wai Jiao Ta Lu — that helped, at least; if he had lived in our ghetto it would have been too much. But he saw Elena at school, for six hours each day. It was horrible.

His name was Fabrice. I had never heard this name before, and I decided on the spot that no more buffoonish name existed. Even more buffoonish was the fact that he had long hair. A most buffoonish buffoon.

Alas, I seemed to be the only one who thought so.

Fabrice appeared to be the leader of the first grade.

My beloved had fallen for power. I felt embarrassed for her.

And strangely, it only made me love her the more.

I never understood why my father seemed so stressed and preoccupied. In Japan his manner had been jovial. In Peking he was another man entirely.

Since his arrival he had worked hard to get the Chinese to reveal the line-up of their cabinet.

I wondered whether this preoccupation made any sense. Obviously, it did to him. But it was hopeless: each time he enquired, the Chinese authorities replied that it was a secret.

He protested this in the most polite manner possible:

"But no other country in the world keeps the names of its cabinet ministers secret!"

His argument had no effect on the authorities.

And so the diplomats posted to Peking were reduced to addressing fictitious, unnamed ministers — an interesting exercise that required a strong capacity for abstraction and an admirable dose of speculative audacity.

One thinks of Stendhal's prayer:

"Oh God, if you exist, have pity on my soul, if I have one."

Communication with the Chinese government was much the same sort of thing.

In fact, the system in place was even more subtle than theology, for it never ceased to confound with its inconsistency. For instance, an official communiqué might contain a phrase like: "The new textile factory in the commune of _____ was inaugurated by the Minister of Industry, Comrade So-and-so . . . "

And all the diplomats in Peking would run for their government listings and fill in, among the twenty blanks, "September 11, 1974: the Minister of Industry is So-and-so . . . "

The political puzzle would get filled in little by little, month by month, but always with an immense margin of uncertainty because the composition of the Chinese cabinet was instability itself. Two months later, without the slightest warning, one would come across another official communiqué which said: "Following the declarations of the Minister of Industry, Comrade Such-and-such . . . "

And one had to start all over again.

The more mystically minded consoled themselves with flights of imagination: "In Peking will eventually be revealed to us the nature of what the Ancients called *deus absconditus . . .*

The others played bridge.

I didn't worry about that sort of thing.

Other matters were more serious.

Specifically this Fabrice, whose prestige grew

before one's eyes, and in whom Elena seemed less and less uninterested.

I didn't ask myself what this boy had that I didn't. I knew what he had.

And that is what I found perplexing: could it be that Elena didn't find that object ridiculous? Could it be that she found it to have some degree of charm? All the evidence pointed that way.

At the age of fourteen I would change my opinion on this point, to my great astonishment. But at seven, such a preference seemed inconceivable.

I concluded with horror that my beloved had lost her mind.

I attempted a desperate gamble. Taking the Italian girl aside, I whispered in her ear about the disability from which Fabrice suffered.

She looked at me with contained hilarity — and it was clearly me, and not the object in question, that inspired it.

I realized that Elena was beyond hope.

I spent the night crying, not because I didn't have such an object, but because my beloved had such bad taste.

At school, a daring teacher dreamed up a project to engage us in something other than making paper airplanes.

He brought the three classes together, and I found myself with Elena and her court.

"Children, I have an idea. We are going to write a story together."

From the start, this proposal made me very uneasy. But I was the only one to react this way. Everyone else was enthused.

"Everyone who knows how to write, go ahead and write your own story. Then we'll choose the best one and make it into a big book with illustrations."

"Yuk," I thought to myself.

This project was supposed to inspire the innumerable illiterates in our classes to learn to write.

Well, if we were going to waste time, I might as well work on a story that interested me.

I embarked on a torrid narrative.

A beautiful Russian princess (why Russian? I still ask myself) was imprisoned, naked, in a mountain of snow. She had long black hair and dark eyes, which fit perfectly with her type of suffering, because the cold forced her to endure dreadful pain. Only her head emerged from the snow, and she saw that there was no one around to save her. There followed a long description of her weeping and suffering. I revelled in it. Eventually another princess arrived on the scene, a *deus ex machina*, who pulled her out and set about warming up her frozen body. I nearly fainted from the voluptuous pleasure of describing how this was accomplished.

I handed in my copy, my face haunted.

For mysterious reasons, it disappeared without a trace. The teacher never even mentioned it.

Yet he read out all the others, which had to do with little pigs, Dalmatians, noses that grew when lies were uttered — in other words, that all had a sense of *déjà vu* about them.

To my great shame, I confess to having forgotten what Elena's was about.

But I haven't forgotten which kid won the contest, and the demagoguery he used to do it.

A Rumanian electoral campaign would have been a model of honesty in comparison.

Fabrice — for of course it was he — had concocted a parable of altruism. The story took place in Africa. A little black boy, faced with the sight of his family dying of hunger, goes in search of food. He heads to the city and becomes very rich. Ten years later he returns to his village, showers his family with food and presents, and builds a hospital.

The teacher introduced this edifying tale to us as follows:

"I have kept the story by Fabrice till last. I don't know what you all will think of it, but it's the one I like best."

And he read out the story, which was received by a chorus of insipid enthusiasm.

"Well, children, I believe it's unanimous."

I can't describe how much this manoeuvre disgusted me.

First of all, I'd found Fabrice's saga silly and sentimental.

"It's so kind-hearted!" I said to myself as I listened to it, with as much distaste as one might say, "It's such propaganda!"

And that adult's spontaneous approval struck me immediately as a guarantee of lousiness. This impression was later confirmed by the blatant ideological manipulation that ensued.

For the rest was consistent with the preceding: vote by acclamation rather than by ballot, triumph of "more-or-less" in the counting, and so on.

And to cap it all: the face of the conqueror arriving on the balcony to salute the voters and treat them to greater details about his plans.

His calm, contented smile!

His cretinous voice explicating his pretty story of courageous villagers!

And, worst of all, the unanimous cries of joy from that herd of little twerps!

The only one not to join in the ululation was Elena, but her evident pride as she looked upon the hero of the day was not much of an improvement.

To tell you the truth, my story's suppression barely hurt at all. My ambitions were martial and amatory. Writing was for others.

However. The unspeakable nice-ness of that young buffoon's story, and the acclaim it received, made me want to puke.

The enormous role of jealousy and malice in my indignation does not detract from the essence of the affair: I was revolted by the public adulation of this story in which fine sentiments took the place of imagination.

From that moment on, I knew that the world of literature was rotten.

The machine had been set in motion.

There were supposed to have been forty children — three classes — working on this project.

In fact, the scribes numbered, at most, only thirty-nine. Because I'd rather have croaked than contributed, even a tiny bit, to this enterprise of public edification.

Say we also exclude the Peruvians and other extraterrestrials who had fallen to Earth among us, who spoke not a word of French. That gives us thirty-four.

From this, we must deduct the mute followers, those eternal packhorses who attend all political systems, and whose thick-headed silence is their substitute for participation. That leaves us with 20 scribes.

Subtract Elena, who never spoke, in keeping with her sphinx-like image. Nineteen.

Subtract nine girls who were in love with Fabrice, and who opened their mouths only to support noisily whatever their long-haired idol might suggest. That brings us down to ten.

Subtract four boys for whom Fabrice was a role-model, and who were left slack-jawed with admiration at his every utterance. Six.

Subtract a Rumanian who, always formal, repeated at the top of his lungs how much he liked the project and how delighted he was to participate. Which was the sum total of his participation. Five.

Subtract two rivals of Fabrice's, who timidly attempted to oppose his ideas and whose every interjection was howled down. Three.

Subtract a very odd child, who only expressed himself by mouthing silently whatever he had to say. Two.

Subtract a boy who claimed, possibly in all sincerity, that he had no imagination at all.

And that is how my rival came to write our collective project all by himself. (Which, in any case, is how the majority of collective creations are produced.)

And that is how we, who were supposed to be stimulated to learn to read and write, learned nothing whatsoever.

The machine rolled on for three months.

As the process advanced, the teacher became aware of certain functional problems in this less and less collective enterprise.

Not that he regretted his idea, since we didn't kill anyone during those three months — in itself a notable success.

Nonetheless, he was quite angry when he understood that this caravan of the dumb had ground to a halt under his very nose. He then ordered all who weren't writing to help illustrate the charming story.

A committee was thus created, composed of some twenty children who were assigned to drawing the admirable deeds of the narrative's hero.

For obscure reasons which nonetheless fit perfectly with the joyously nourishing theme of the humanitarian fable, the teacher decreed that our pictorial masterpiece would be executed with pieces of raw potato, dipped in Indian ink.

This idea, doubtless intended to be avant-garde, was doubly grotesque given that the price of potatoes was far higher in Peking than the price of paintbrushes.

The committee members were divided between (a) artists and painters, and (b) peeler and cutters of potatoes. I declared myself to be without talent and joined the corps of peelers, where in my secret rage I devised numerous techniques for sabotaging potatoes. Any means was fair to me: cutting them too thin, or cutting them oddly, or even taking my heroism so far as to eat the tubers to make them disappear.

I have never set foot in a Ministry of Culture, but when I try to imagine one I am transported to that class in the City of Electric Fans, with its ten peelers of potatoes, ten painters improvising blobs on paper, nineteen intellectuals without any perceivable function, and a guru writing a noble collective story all by himself.

◆

If China is almost absent from these pages, it is not because it doesn't interest me. One doesn't have to be an adult to be infected with the virus that may be called sinomania, sinopathy, and even sinolatry — terms that can be adapted depending on how one wants to use the country in question. We are only now beginning to understand that to take an interest in China is to take interest in oneself. For very strange reasons, which doubtless have to do with China's vastness, its antiquity, its unequalled degree of civilization, its arrogance, its monstrous refinement, its legendary cruelty, its squalor, its paradoxes more unplumbable than those of other countries, its silence, its mythic beauty, its completeness, its reputation for intelligence, its creeping hegemony, its permanence, the passion it excites, the freedom of interpretation its mystery allows, and finally and above all the degree to which it remains misunderstood — for all of these reasons, many of them difficult to admit, individuals tend to feel an inner compulsion to identify themselves with China, and even worse to see China as their geographic manifestation.

And like those discreet establishments where solid citizens go to act out their least acceptable fantasies, China is the place where one is permitted to deliver oneself to one's basest instincts, namely to talk about oneself. For, by a highly convenient process of distortion, talking about China nearly always turns into talking about oneself (the exceptions can be counted on the fingers of one hand). It is the source of the pretentiousness I mentioned earlier; whether disguised as criticism or the wildest forms of mortification, the discourse never strays far from the first person singular.

Children are even more egocentric than adults, and that is why China fascinated me from the moment I set foot there at the age of five. For this fascination, which even the simplest souls can share, is not fanciful: the fact is that we are all Chinese. In different degrees, certainly: everyone has some level of China in them, the same way everyone has some measure of cholesterol in their blood or narcissism in their gaze. All civilizations are interpretations of the Chinese model. We ought to add the construction "prehistory/China/civilization" to our reservoir of intra-referential phrases since it is impossible to utter any one of these words without including the two others.

And yet, China is almost absent from these pages. A multitude of explanations might be invoked: that China is all the more present because it is so little mentioned; that this story is an evocation of childhood, and, in a certain sense, everyone's childhood takes place in China; that the Middle Kingdom is too intimate a part of humanity for me to dare describe it too closely; that in this double voyage — through childhood and China — words are especially fragile. These explanations would not be dishonest, and there are certainly people who would buy them.

Yet I reject them for the sorriest of explanations, which is that the story happens in China, but just barely. I would greatly prefer that the story didn't take place there, for a long list of reasons. It would be comforting to know that this China no longer exists, that somehow it has gone away and what remains on Eurasia's edge is an enormous nation without a soul, without a name, and therefore without real suffering. Alas, I can't make this argument. Against all hope, this sordid country is indeed still China.

What I'm challenging is the presence of foreigners there. Let's be clear about what the term "to be present" means. Certainly, we lived in Peking, but can one really talk about being present in China when one is so carefully isolated from the Chinese? When access to the immense majority of the country is forbidden? When contacts with the population are impossible?

In three years, we had real communication with only one Chinese: the embassy's interpreter, a charming man with the singular name of Chang. He spoke a delightful French full of phonetic approximations: for example, he often spoke about *"l'eau très froide"* (the very cold water). It took us a little while to understand why Mr. Chang began his sentences so frequently with l'eau très froide — it was how he had heard *"autrefois"* (formerly). The stories he told about cold water were, in any case, engrossing, and one felt how keenly he was gripped by nostalgia. Unfortunately, all this cold water got Mr. Chang noticed. One day he disappeared, or rather evaporated without leaving the faintest trace — as if he had never existed.

His fate can only be guessed at, and all guesses are equally valid.

He was replaced just as suddenly by an unbending, ill-natured woman with the singular name of Chang. But while Mr. Chang had been a mister, his replacement would not tolerate any other form of address than "Comrade." A "Mrs. Chang" or "Miss Chang" was summarily corrected as if it were a gross grammatical error. One day my mother asked, "Comrade Chang, how did one address a Chinese person before? Was there an equivalent of Mister or Missus?"

"Chinese people are called Comrade," responded the interpreter, implacably.

"Yes of course, nowadays," said my naive mother. "But before . . . You know, before."

"There is no before," stated Comrade Chang, as abrupt as ever.

We got the message.

China had no past.

There simply was no longer any question of l'eau très froide.

In the streets, the Chinese shied away from us as if we were infected with some contagious disease. And as for the domestic servants that the authorities assigned to foreigners, their relations with us were circumspect to a degree difficult to imagine — which at least inclines one to believe that they weren't spies.

Our cook, who had the singular name of Chang, was astonishingly decent to us, doubtless because it gave him access to a world of food that a famished China could only dream of. Chang was obsessed with the idea of stuffing full these three little Occidentals that had been assigned him. He was present at all the meals we ate without our parents, which is to say most of them, and he watched us eat with an expression of extreme gravity on his austere old face, as if the most important questions in the universe were being decided on our plates. He never said anything except for two words: "Much eat," a sacred formula that he used sparingly and with the solemnity of an incantation. Our appetites could be read on his face, from the satisfaction of a mission accomplished to a painful anguish. Chang the Cook loved us. And if he forced us to eat, it was because the authorities wouldn't let him express his tenderness any other way: food was the only authorized language between the foreigners and the Chinese.

Apart from that, there were the markets, where I rode my horse to buy caramels, cock-eyed goldfish, Indian ink, and other marvels, but where communication was limited to exchanges of money.

And I can certify that was all the exchange that occurred.

Under the circumstances, I can only conclude with this: this story happened in China to the extent that it was permitted to do so — which is to say very little.

It is a ghetto story, a tale of double exile: exile from our native country (which for me was Japan, since I was convinced that I was Japanese), and exile from the

China which surrounded us but from which we were cut off, by virtue of our status as profoundly unwanted guests.

Make no mistake, however: in the end, China has the same weight in these pages as the Black Death had in Bocaccio's *Decameron:* though hardly mentioned, it RAGES throughout.

Elena had never been accessible to me. And since the advent of Fabrice, she escaped me more and more.

I no longer had any idea how to catch her attention. I was tempted to tell her my theory about China's electric fans, but intuition told me that she would react the same way as she had with the horse: she would shrug and ignore me.

I blessed the fate that decreed Fabrice would live in Wai Jiao Ta Lu. And I blessed my beloved's mother, who forbade her children to set foot outside San Li Tun.

Getting from one ghetto to another was, in fact, no problem at all. By bicycle it took a quarter of an hour. I often made the trip because there was a shop in Wai Jiao Ta Lu that sold a vile brand of Chinese caramels, pure bacteria, that seemed to me the most heavenly confections under the sun.

I noticed that in his three months of flirtation, Fabrice had never visited San Li Tun.

That gave me what I hoped was a cunning idea. After school one day, I casually asked the Italian girl:

"Is Fabrice in love with you?

"Yes," she replied indifferently, as if it went without saying.

"And do you love him?

"I'm his fiancée."

"His fiancée! So you must see him a lot."

"Every day, at school."

"No, not every day. Not Saturday and Sunday."

Distant silence.

"And you don't see him in the evenings either. Even if that's when fiancés are really supposed to see each other. To go to the cinema."

"There is no cinema in San Li Tun."

"There's a cinema at the Alliance Française, near Wai Jiao Ta Lu."

"Mama doesn't let me leave San Li Tun."

"So why doesn't Fabrice come and visit you here?"

Silence.

"It only takes a quarter of an hour by bike. I do it almost every day."

"Mama says it's dangerous to go out."

"So? Is Fabrice afraid? I go out all the time."

"His parents won't let him."

"And he does what he's told?"

Silence.

"I'll ask him to come and see me tomorrow. He'll do it, you'll see. He does everything I ask him to do."

"Nah! If he really loves you he has to think of it himself. Otherwise it doesn't count."

"He loves me."

"So why doesn't he come?"

Silence.

"Perhaps he has another fiancée in Wai Jiao Ta Lu," I said, as if tossing out a hypothesis.

Elena laughed disdainfully.

"The other girls there aren't nearly as pretty as I am."

"How do you know? They don't all go to the French School. The English girls, for instance."

"The English girls!" she laughed, as if the mere mention removed them from the running.

"Yes, the English girls. What about Lady Godiva?"

Elena's eyes flashed question marks at me. I explained that English girls customarily went about naked, on horseback, clothed only in their exceedingly long tresses.

"But there aren't any horses in the ghettos," said Elena coldly.

"You think an English girl would let that get in her way?"

My beloved left me at a rapid pace. It was the first time I'd seen her walk quickly.

Her face had not shown any trace of discomfort, but I was certain that at the very least I'd nicked her pride, if not the heart whose existence I could never confirm.

It felt like a stunning triumph.

◆

I never heard anything more about my rival's putative bigamy. All I knew was that Elena broke off her engagement on the following day.

She carried it off with exemplary indifference. I was very proud of her lack of sentiment.

The prestige of the long-haired seducer had taken a savage blow.

I revelled in it.

For the second time I blessed Chinese communism.

With the approach of winter, the war intensified.

We knew that once the frost came, we would all be given picks and conscripted, *volens nolens*, to break up the sheets of ice that coated the ground and immobilized the vehicles.

We therefore needed to spit out in advance our quota of aggression.

All methods of warfare were fair.

We were particularly proud of our new detachment, which we dubbed the "Puke Patrol."

For we had discovered that some of our number had been born with special abilities: the fairies who had perched on their cribs had made them capable of vomiting almost at will. They had only to ingest something, and they were immediately ready to expel it.

One had to admire them.

Most used the classic method of the finger down

the throat. But a few were much more impressive: they expelled through sheer force of will. Some extraordinary spiritual power gave them access to the emetic centers of the brain: they merely concentrated a little and the deed was done.

Maintaining the Puke Patrol was rather like looking after certain airplanes: it was sometimes necessary to refuel them in mid-air. Dry-heaving, we recognized, was of no military value.

Our least useful members were assigned to forage for emetic propellant, more specifically to steal easily eaten food from the Chinese cooks. The adults must have noted significant disappearances of cookies, raisins, processed cheese, condensed milk, chocolate, and, above all, instant coffee and oil — for we had discovered the philosopher's stone of vomiting: a mixture of salad oil and instant coffee. It came back up the quickest.

(A heart-warming detail: not one of these provisions was available in Peking. Our parents had to go to Hong Kong for supplies every three months, and these trips were expensive. Our puking cost them dearly.)

The essential criterion was weight: the material had to be easy to transport, which immediately eliminated all food in glass jars. Those who carried the supplies were called "containers." A vomiter always had to escorted by at least one container. Some beautiful friendships blossomed from these complementary activities.

For the Germans, there was no torture more terrible. A dunking in the Secret Weapon often made them cry, but left them their dignity. Being puked on left their dignity in shreds: they shrieked with horror as if touched by sulphuric acid. One of them was actually so revolted that he himself threw up, to our huge delight.

Of course, the health of the vomiters deteriorated very quickly. But their vocation won them such praise that they accepted the physical damage with serenity.

In my eyes, their prestige was unequalled. I dreamed of joining the Patrol. Alas, I hadn't the necessary physical gift. I could swallow the horrible philosopher's stone all I liked, but the desired result never arose.

Yet I still absolutely needed to perform some stunning deed. Without one, Elena would never want me.

I prepared myself in great secrecy.

Meanwhile, back at the school, my beloved had returned to her ambulant solitude.

I now knew that she wasn't untouchable. So I stuck to her at every recess, unaware of this tactic's resounding stupidity.

I walked at her side, talking to her. She scarcely seemed to hear me. That hardly mattered to me: her beauty prevented me from thinking straight.

For Elena truly was superb. On the one hand, her Italian grace, exquisite in its civilization, elegance, and intelligence; on the other, her mother's Amerindian blood, imbued with all the lyric savagery of human sacrifice and other barbarities that my naive imagination still attached to it. My beloved's glance was a cocktail of curare and Raphael: something to knock one dead in a second.

And she knew it.

That day, in the school's playground, I could not prevent myself from uttering that classic line that, in my mouth, was a newly minted expression of unlimited sincerity:

"You're so beautiful that I would do anything for you."

"I've been told that before," she observed indifferently.

"But I really mean it," I rushed on, conscious of the sting in my response's tail, given the recent Fabrice business.

I was treated to an ironic little look that seemed to say, "Do you really think that hurt me?"

Because it had to be admitted: although the French boy had clearly been crushed by the break-up, the Italian girl had felt nothing at all, proving that she had never loved her fiancé.

"So you'd do anything for me?" she continued in an amused tone of voice.

"Yes!" I said, hoping she'd order me to do something ghastly.

"Well then, I want you to run around the schoolyard twenty times without stopping."

The test seemed a trivial one. I started immediately. I ran like a bullet, deliriously happy. My enthusiasm began to sink around the tenth lap. It fell further when I noted that Elena wasn't watching me, and for good reason: some young buffoon had started talking to her.

I fulfilled my contract, nonetheless, too faithful — too stupid — to lie, and presented myself before the fair one and the third party.

"Done," I said.

"Done what?" she asked me.

"I ran around the schoolyard twenty times."

"Ah. I'd forgotten. Do it again, I didn't see you."

I began immediately. I saw that she was hardly watching. But nothing could have stopped me. I discovered that I was glad to run: the motion of my strides gave my passion a noble means of expression, and although I didn't win what I'd hoped for, my heart leapt within me.

"Done."

"Good," she said negligently. "Twenty more."

Neither she nor the buffoon appeared to see me at all.

I ran. I repeated to myself, ecstasy crowding the edges of my consciousness, that I was running for love. At the same time, I felt my asthma taking hold of me. Worse: I remembered telling Elena that I was asthmatic. She hadn't known what it was, and I had explained it to her: for once, she had listened with interest.

So she had given me the order in full knowledge of what she was doing.

After the sixtieth lap, I returned to my beloved.

"Do it again."

"You remember what I told you?" I asked timidly.

"What about?"

"The asthma."

"Do you think I'd ask you to run if I didn't remember?" she replied with absolute indifference.

Crushed, I ran.

My grip on reality began to loosen.

I ran on. A voice soliloquized in my head: "You want me to sabotage myself for you? You're on! It's worthy of you and worthy of me. Just watch how far I'll take this."

Sabotage was a word with all kinds of resonance for me. I knew nothing of etymology, but in sabotage I heard "*sabot*," the French word for horseshoe — and that was perfect, because my horse's legs were nothing less than extensions of myself. Elena wanted me to sabotage myself for her: what better way than to extinguish myself in a mad gallop? So I ran, imagining that the ground was my body and that I was trampling it at the fair one's command, and that I would gallop until my body's gave up the ghost. I smiled at this magnificent prospect and I accelerated my sabotage by running ever faster.

My endurance astonished me. All that intense biking — galloping — had given me terrific stamina, despite the asthma. Nonetheless, I could feel the attack coming on. Breath came harder and harder, and the pain was becoming vicious.

The Italian girl lifted not an eye to my running, but nothing, nothing in this world could stop me.

She had devised this test because she knew I had asthma, but she had no idea how perfect a choice she'd made. Asthma? A detail, a mere technical defect in my seven-year-old carcass.

What counted was that she had asked me to run. And motion was my horse's coat of arms, the virtue I honored above all others, — pure speed, not to save time but to escape from time, from gluey chronology, from the mire of joyless thoughts, sad bodies, obese lives, and flabby ruminations.

You, Elena, so beautiful, so unhurried, perhaps because only you could allow yourself that luxury. You whose walk was always leisurely, as if to let us admire you that little bit longer; doubtless without knowing it, you had ordered me to be myself; that is, to reduce myself to motion, unthinking, a cannonball drunk with its passage through the air.

On the eighty-eighth lap, the light began to dim. The faces of the children grew dark. The last of the fans stopped turning. My lungs exploded with pain.

Blackout.

When I came to, I was at home in bed. My mother asked what had happened.

"The children said you wouldn't stop running."

"I was exercising."

"Promise me you'll never do that again."

"I can't."

"Why?"

In my weakened state, I ended up telling her everything. I wanted at least one person to be aware of my heroism. I could accepting dying for love, but not anonymously.

My mother then launched into an explanation of the laws of the universe. She said that this world contained certain people who were very wicked and, at the same time, very appealing. She assured me that if I wanted to make one of them love me, there was only one way to go about it: I had to be equally wicked.

"You have to do the same to her that she is doing to you."

"But that's impossible. She doesn't love me."

"Be like her, and she will."

The sentence brooked no appeal. I found it absurd: I loved Elena because she was so unlike me. What sense was there in a love like a mirror? I resolved, nonetheless, to try out my mother's plan of attack, at least as an experiment. Surely the person who had taught me to tie my shoelaces must know something.

A new turn of events proved favorable to this tactic.

In the course of a battle, the Allies had captured the head of the German army, a certain Werner, whom we had never managed to lay hands on before and who, in our eyes, was Evil incarnate.

We exulted. Werner was in for it. He deserved a special treatment.

Which is to say, the works.

The captured general was trussed up like a chicken and gagged with dampened cotton wool. (Dampened with the Secret Weapon, of course.)

After two hours of an appropriately menacing verbal gang-bang, Werner was carried to the top of the fire escape and left hanging in the void for a quarter of an hour, at the end of a strong cord. By the way he twisted and turned, one perceived that he was terrified of heights.

When we pulled him back up to the platform, his face had gone all blue.

He was then taken back down and tortured in the more classic fashion. He was submerged in the Secret Weapon for a whole minute, after which he was delivered to the tender mercies of the Puke Patrol, fully loaded for action.

This was all excellent, but our aggression was still unsatisfied. We had run out of things to do to him.

My moment had arrived.

"Wait," I murmured, my voice so solemn that it imposed silence.

The other children looked at me with a certain benevolence because I was the baby of the army. But what I did next elevated me to the rank of a military monster.

I walked to the prone German general's head.

102

As a musician might declare "*Allegro ma non troppo*" before a piece, I announced:

"Standing, no hands."

My voice was as matter-of-fact as Elena's.

And I did it, right between Werner's eyes, which rolled with humiliation.

A hushed murmur ran through the assembly. No one had ever seen this before.

I left, walking unhurriedly. My face showed nothing. I was delirious with pride.

I felt struck by glory as others are struck by lightning. The smallest of my gestures seemed monumental to me. Life had become a victory march. I sneered at the Peking sky. My horse would be pleased with me.

Night had fallen. The German boy was left for dead. My exploit had so impressed the Allies that they had forgotten about him.

His parents found him the following morning soaked in the Secret Weapon, with patches of vomit frozen in his clothes and hair.

The boy caught the cold of the century, but it was nothing compared with the psychological damage he'd sustained. One detail in his story even caused his family to think he'd lost his sanity.

East—west tension in San Li Tun had reached its apogee.

My pride knew no limits.

◆

My renown spread like a wildfire throughout the French school.

Only a week earlier, I had blacked out from an asthma attack. Now my monstrous talents had been revealed. Without doubt, I was a somebody.

My beloved heard all this.

In conformance with my battle plan, I affected to no longer be aware of her existence.

One day, in the schoolyard, she walked up to me — miracle without precedent!

She asked me with a vague puzzlement:

"Is it true what they say?"

"What do they say?" I said without looking at her.

"That you do it standing up, no hands, and that you can aim?"

"It's true," I answered disdainfully, as if it were something perfectly ordinary.

And I kept walking, my pace relaxed, without another word.

Feigning such indifference was a sore trial, yet the obvious effectiveness of the tactic gave me the strength to continue.

The snow arrived.

It was my third winter in the City of Electric Fans. As usual, my nose started expelling blood in prodigious quantities.

The snow was the only thing that could hide the

ugliness of Peking, at least for the first ten hours of its existence. All that Chinese concrete — without doubt the ugliest in the world — disappeared beneath the blinding whiteness. Blinding in the double sense of the term: while the snow blurred the barrier between earth and sky, its perfect whiteness also made it possible to imagine that immense fields of nothingness had invaded parts of the city — and in Peking, far from being an absence of something, nothingness was like redemption.

The delicate juxtaposition of void and fullness made San Li Tun look like a woodcut.

One felt almost as if one were in China.

Ten hours later, the metamorphosis reversed itself.

The concrete spread across the snow, and ugliness spread across beauty.

Order was re-established.

The snow had changed nothing. It is striking how ugliness always wins out. Scarcely had the snowflakes landed on the Peking ground before they became hideous.

I don't like metaphors. So I will not say that a city snowfall is a metaphor for life. I don't have to: everyone already knows it.

One day I will write a book called *City Snow*. It will be the saddest book in literary history. But no, I won't write it after all. Why write about the horrors that everyone is familiar with?

So let's get it over with once and for all: the fact that something so lovely, so velvety-soft, so gentle, so swirling, so light as the snow can turn itself so quickly into its opposite — a grey, sticky, compacted, heavy, rough mess — is one of nature's nasty tricks that I'll never get used to.

I hated winter in Peking. I detested having to take up scraper and rake to break up the frozen snow that brought the ghetto to a standstill.

And the other conscripted children felt as I did. The war was suspended until spring thaw — which might seem a little paradoxical.

To reimburse us for our street-cleaning efforts, the adults took us on Sundays to skate on the lake of the Summer Palace. For me, these expeditions seemed too beautiful to be real. The immense body of frozen water, which reflected the boreal light and screeched with the sound of the skates, put me in such a state of ecstasy that it gave me headaches. I had no immunity against beauty.

On the other days, we were handed shovels and picks as soon as we got back from school.

All of the children were conscripted, with two notable exceptions: Elena, and the oh-so-precious Claudio.

Their mother had decreed that her little ones were too fragile for such rough work.

In the fair one's case there was no protest.

But her big brother's exemption only added to his remarkable lack of popularity.

Bundled up in an old coat and a Chinese goatskin hat, I set about smashing up the ice. Since San Li Tun so closely resembled a penitentiary, I felt like I had been condemned to hard labor.

Later on, when I had become a Nobel Prize winner in medicine or a martyr, I would tell of how I had served time in the prison camps of Peking following my military exploits.

All I lacked was a ball and chain.

An apparition materialized before me: a delicate creature dressed in a white cloak, her long black hair flowing freely down from a little beret of white felt.

She was so beautiful I thought I'd faint, which would have been a useful way out.

But my battle plan had not changed. I pretended not to see her and whacked the frozen ground fiercely with my pick.

"I'm bored. Come and play with me."

Her voice was as soft as ermine.

"Can't you see I'm working?" I asked as disagreeably as possible.

"There are lots of other children who can do it," she said, gesturing at the multitude of kids who worked the ice around us.

"I don't mind getting my hands dirty. I'd be ashamed to sit around doing nothing."

I was actually more ashamed to be saying such a thing, but such was my battle plan.

Silence. I continued my labor.

Elena's next move was dramatic.

"Give me your pick," she said.

Stupefied, I stared at her without saying a word.

She took hold of my pick, raised it in the air with touching effort and let it drop to the ground. Then she made as if to do it again.

I felt I'd never seen such blasphemy. I grabbed the tool from her and rasped:

"No! Not you!"

"Why?" she asked, an angelic look on her face and the same ermine voice.

I didn't answer and resumed breaking up the ice, eyes to the ground.

My beloved walked off slowly, fully conscious of having scored a point.

School clearly brought out the importance of war as catharsis.

War was about destroying the enemy. School was about settling scores among the Allies.

War served to purge the aggression accumulated by everyday life. School served to distill the aggression accumulated by war.

All things considered, we were reasonably happy.

However, the Werner business had stirred up the adults.

The East German parents informed the parents of

the Allies that this time their children had gone too far.

Since they could not force the guilty to be punished, they demanded an armistice. If this demand were not met, "diplomatic reprisals" would follow.

Our parents gave in immediately. We were ashamed of them.

A delegation of adults came to admonish our generals. Our hot war, they stated, was incompatible with the Cold War. It would have to stop. There was no room for discussion. Food, beds and cars were all in adult hands. There was no way we could disobey.

Nonetheless, our generals had the guts to state that we still needed enemies.

"Why?"

"For war, of course!"

We never dreamed that anyone could ask anything so obvious.

"Do you really need a war?" asked the adults, approaching the end of their tethers.

Recognizing their advanced stage of degeneration, we didn't answer.

In any case, hostilities were suspended so long as the city remained frozen.

The parents believed that we had signed the armistice. In fact, we were waiting for Armageddon.

That winter was a sore trial.

A trial for the Chinese, who were dying of cold —

something which, it must be admitted, didn't concern the children of San Li Tun.

A trial for the children of San Li Tun, condemned to break up the ice during their spare time.

A trial for our martial impulses, contained until spring: war seemed like the Holy Grail. But the sheets of ice to be cleared grew each night, and the month of March seemed to be receding from us. One might have thought that smashing the ice would ease our thirst for violence: on the contrary, it was gasoline on the flames. Some blocks of ice were so hard that, in order to give ourselves more strength, we imagined ourselves slamming our picks into German flesh.

A trial for me, finally, on all fronts of my campaign. I followed my battle plan to the letter, and was as cold with Elena as the Peking winter.

And the more I stuck to my plan, the more the Italian girl gazed upon me with her large, tender eyes. Yes, tender. I would never have imagined that one day she would wear such an expression. And for me!

How could I have known that the two of us belonged to two different species. Elena was one of those who loves more strongly the colder someone is to her. I was the opposite: the more I felt myself loved, the more I loved.

Granted, I hadn't needed the fair one's tender gaze to fall in love with her. But her new attitude increased my passion tenfold.

Love was beginning to make me delirious. At night in my bed, I saw again the gentle eyes that had caressed me, and I fell into a semi-swoon, trembling and half-paralyzed.

I asked myself what I was waiting for. I no longer doubted her love. All I had to do was respond to it.

I didn't dare. I felt my passion had assumed formidable proportions. Declaring it would take me beyond my depth: it would require something more than language, something beyond my mind's reach, something I might have glimpsed but not comprehended.

So I stuck to my battle plan. Though ever more painful, at least its execution presented no mysteries.

Elena's stares were becoming more and more insistent, more and more lacerating. The less a face is made for gentleness, the more its gentleness is disturbing — and the gentleness in her Sagittarian eyes and the tenderness on her wicked mouth took my breath away.

When that happened I needed additional armor, and I became as icy and cutting as a hailstorm — at which the fair one's gaze would soften in even greater adoration.

It was unbearable.

There is nothing so cruel as snow.

The snow, ugly and grey as it was in the City of Electric Fans, was still snow.

The snow, cast in my illiterate fantasies as the perfect image of love, and not without reason.

The snow, totally without innocence beneath its guileless beatitude.

The snow, wherein I read things that made me very hot and then very cold.

The snow, hard and dirty, which I ended up eating in the vain hope of finding an answer.

The snow, exploded water, frozen sand, salt without sodium born not of earth but of sky, flinty-tasting, sap-textured, cold-smelling, white-pigmented, the only color that falls from the clouds.

The snow, that deadens everything — noises, tumbles, time — and thereby calls into question all that is eternal and immutable, like blood and light and illusions.

The snow, History's original parchment, on which so many paths, so many merciless pursuits have been written; the snow that was therefore the first literary genre, an immense book set at ground-level, filled with nothing but hunting spoors and enemy itineraries, a sort of geographic epic in which even the most minor markings become enigmas — is this my brother's footprint, or his murderer's?

There remains not one fragment of this unending, unfinished book, which might be called The Biggest Book in the World — unlike those of the Library of Alexandria, all of its texts have melted. But something must have remained with us, a distant memory that reappears with each new snowfall, the vague anguish of a blank page that sparks the terrible urge to tread its virgin spaces, the instinctive urge for explanation that arises the moment one discovers the trace of an Other.

When you get right down to it, snow invented mystery. And in doing so, it invented poetry, the woodcut, the question mark — and that great foot-race that is love.

The snow, that false shroud, that great empty ideogram in which I deciphered the infinity of sensations that I wanted to offer my beloved.

I did not care whether my desire was pure or impure. I knew only that the snow made Elena more irresistible, my beautiful secret more breathtaking, and my battle plan more unbearable.

Never was spring more eagerly awaited.

Beware of flowers.

Especially in Peking.

I knew communism as a phenomenon of electric fans. The historical episode known as the One Hundred Flowers Campaign meant no more to me than Ho Chi Minh or Wittgenstein.

Yet even had I known, warnings are useless when it comes to flowers: one always falls into the trap.

What is a flower? A giant sexual organ in its Sunday best. This truth has been known for a long time, yet, over-aged adolescents that we are, we persist in speaking sentimental drivel about the delicacy of flowers. We construct idiotic phrases like "So-and-so is in the flower of his youth," which is as absurd as saying "in the vagina of his youth."

There were very few flowers in San Li Tun, and they were all ugly. But they were flowers all the same.

Hothouse flowers are as pretty as fashion models, but they have no scent. The flowers of the ghetto seemed curiously garbed; some were as scruffy as peasants visiting the big city, while others seemed as garish as urbanites in a farmer's field. All seemed beside the point.

Still, if one closed one's eyes, stopped one's ears, and stuck one's nose into their corollas, one wanted to cry. What was it, deep within the most unremarkable of flowers with their pleasantly uninteresting scents? What could it be that was so heart-rending? Why that nostalgia for memories that aren't one's own, for gardens one has never known, for imperial beauties one has never heard of? Why was it that the Cultural Revolution never forbade flowers to smell like flowers?

With the ghetto in flower, the war could finally begin again.

This time it was a debacle, in all senses of the word.

In 1972, the adults had annexed our war. It hadn't bothered us in the slightest.

In the spring of 1975, they sabotaged it. It broke our hearts.

Scarcely had the ice melted and our forced labor ceased, scarcely had we resumed combat with ecstasy and enthusiasm, when our angry parents broke up the party:

"What about the armistice?"

"We never signed anything."

"So you need signatures? Fine. Leave it to us."

It was the most surreal of nightmares, and the peace treaty they typed up was as convoluted as any in history.

They summoned the generals of the opposing forces to a "negotiating table" at which there was nothing to negotiate. They read aloud a French text and a German text; we could understand neither.

All we had was the right to sign.

Thanks to that collective humiliation, we felt a profound sympathy for our enemies. And visibly, it was reciprocated.

Even Werner, who was the cause of this travesty of an armistice, looked disgusted by it.

At the end of the operetta-like ceremony, the adults thought it a nice touch to make a toast with fizzy lemonade, served in champagne glasses. They smiled, happy and relieved. The secretary of the East German embassy, an ill-dressed but affable Aryan, sang a little song.

And thus it was that after annexing our war, the adults annexed our peace.

We were embarrassed for them.

◆

The paradoxical result of this artificial treaty was a mutual infatuation.

The former enemies fell into each other's arms, weeping with anger at their elders.

Never had East Germans been so loved around the world.

Werner sobbed. We hugged him: he had spilled the beans, but it had been a fair fight.

Excuse the redundancy: it was a fight, and therefore necessarily fair.

The nostalgia began there and then. In English, we exchanged happy memories of combat and torture. One might have mistaken it for the kiss-and-make-up scene in an American movie.

The first — no, the only — thing to do was to find a new enemy.

Not just any enemy: there were criteria that had to be satisfied.

The first was geographic: the nation had to be present in San Li Tun.

The second was historic: one could not fight against former Allies. Granted, one can only be betrayed by one's own; and granted, there is nobody more dangerous than one's friends. But one can't attack a brother; one can't pick a fight with someone who, on the frontlines, puked at your side or peed in the same wash basin. That would be a spiritual crime.

The third criterion verged on the irrational: the enemy had to have something detestable about him. Which meant that anything was possible.

Some suggested the Albanians or the Bulgarians, arguing somewhat limply that they were communists. The suggestion got no votes: we'd already tried communists, and see where it had got us.

"How about the Peruvians," said someone.

"Why hate a Peruvian?" asked another — a question with a beautiful metaphysical simplicity.

"Because they don't speak our language," answered an exile from distant Babel.

Clearly, a good reason.

A budding federalist observed that if such were our criterion then war could be declared on three-quarters of the ghetto, and on China itself for that matter.

"Okay, it's a good reason, but it's not enough."

We continued this dissection of nationalities until I had a flash of inspiration:

"The Nepalese!" I exclaimed.

"Why hate a Nepalese?"

To this question, worthy of a Montesquieu, I had a monumental response:

"Because it's the only country in the world without a rectangular flag."

A scandalized silence descended on the assembly.

"Is that true?" asked a voice already hoarse with anger.

I launched into a description of the Nepalese flag, an assemblage of triangles cut in half on the long side.

War was declared on the Nepalese immediately.

"The bastards!"

"We'll teach those Nepalese not to have a rectangular flag like everyone else!"

"Who do these Nepalese think they are!"

Our hatred was in good working order.

The East Germans were as outraged as the rest of us. They asked to join the Allies in this marvellous crusade against non-rectangular flags. We were only too happy to enlist them. To fight at the side of someone we had beaten up and tortured would be a moving experience.

The Nepalese, however, proved themselves to be exceptional enemies.

They were far less numerous than the East Germans. In the beginning, we found this a positive attribute. It never occurred to us that one might feel shame over such disproportion. In fact, this numerical superiority was rather agreeable.

Their average age was greater than ours. Some were as old as fifteen, on the verge of senility. Which was another good reason to hate them.

Our declaration of war was of unequalled clarity: the first two Nepalese we came across found themselves assaulted by sixty children.

When we let them go, they were covered in cuts and bruises.

These unfortunate little mountain people, only seven of them at the most and only recently down from their Himalayas, understood nothing of the situation.

Nonetheless, the children of Kathmandu held council. They adopted the only policy possible: combat — in view of our methods, they understood that diplomacy and negotiation were of no use.

Perhaps I should point out that the behavior of the kids of San Li Tun was the absolute negation of the laws of heredity. Our parents' job was to reduce international tension as much as possible. Whereas we did just the opposite. (Go have children yourself, and see where it gets you.)

We were not only negators but innovators: an alliance so powerful, a war so global, all of this against a poor little country of no ideological significance or influence — that was original.

And without being aware of it, we were abetting Chinese foreign policy. While Mao's soldiers dug further into Tibet, we had opened a second front in the mountains. The Himalayas were given no quarter.

But the Nepalese astonished us. We discovered that they were redoubtable soldiers: their brutality outclassed anything we had seen in three years of war with the East Germans, who were far from being sissies.

The children of Kathmandu unleashed kicks and

punches of unequalled energy and precision. The seven of them proved a formidable enemy.

We were too young to know something that History has proved over and over again: when it comes to violence, no other continent even begins to rival Asia.

It was a tight corner, but we were not unhappy to be in it.

Elena stayed aloof from the battleground.

When I was older I happened to read an obscure story, something about a war between Greeks and Trojans. The fact that they fought over a superb creature named Helen made me grin at the time, I assure you.

Obviously, the parallel wasn't perfect. The war of San Li Tun did not break out because of Elena. She never even wanted to be involved in it.

In a strange way, the *Iliad* actually told me less about San Li Tun than the ghetto taught me about the *Iliad*. To begin with, I doubt I would have been so partial to the *Iliad* if I had never taken part in the war. For me, the experience pre-dated the myth, and I dare say even clarified certain points about it. In particular, it helped me understand the character of Helen.

Is there a story more flattering to a woman than the *Iliad*? Two civilizations tear each other's guts out, without mercy and unto death, the Gods intervene, military intelligence wins its spurs, a world disappears — and all for what? For a beautiful woman.

The story makes it easy to imagine the coquette preening before her friends:

"Yes, my dears, genocide and several acts of divine intervention, for me alone! And I did nothing to deserve it. What can I say? I'm beautiful, and there's nothing I can do about it."

Each re-telling of the myth reverberates with Helen's outrageous uselessness; she becomes the caricature of a ravishing egoist, finding the bloodshed in her name appropriate and even charming.

In my case, however, I met and fell for the fair Helen while I was already at war. And that is why I have another vision of the *Iliad*. Having seen what Elena was like, and how she reacted, I am inclined to believe that her ancient namesake was much like her.

For instance, I think Helen was bored by the Trojan War, to a degree hard to imagine. I doubt she took any pride in it: that would have rendered too much honor to the human armies.

I think she stayed far above the story and instead gazed at herself in the mirror.

I think she had a need to be admired — and never mind if the stares were those of warriors or peace-keepers. What counted was that these looks spoke of her, and her alone, not those who directed them at her.

And I think she needed to be loved. Not *to* love: that wasn't in her repertoire. Each to her own specialty.

121

Did she love Paris? I would be astonished if that were so. But she loved Paris's loving her, and cared little about anything else he might have to offer.

So, what was the Trojan War? A monstrous, blood-drenched, dishonorable, and unjust act of barbarism, perpetrated in the name of a beauty who didn't give a damn.

All wars are Trojan Wars, as are all noble causes pursued for the sake of beauties who don't give a damn.

The only sincerity in war is that which isn't said: the reason people make war is that people like it and because it is an agreeable pastime. And noble causes with beautiful faces are never hard to find.

Helen had good reason, therefore, not to feel implicated and to look at herself in the mirror.

And as for the Helen whom I loved in Peking in 1974, I greatly admire her still.

Too many people think they want war, when all they actually crave is a duel. The *Iliad* sometimes seems like a collection of personal rivalries: each hero finds in the rival camp his tailor-made enemy, the one who will obsess him until he has annihilated him, or vice versa. That is not war: that is love, with all its pride and individualism. Who doesn't dream of a good scrap with some eternal enemy, a foe of one's own, an adversary worthy of oneself?

Of all the struggles I took part in during my time in San Li Tun, the one that best prepared me for reading the *Iliad* was my love for Elena. Among so many confused assaults and mêlées, she provided my one instance of single combat, the joust in keeping with my highest aspirations.

It wasn't the hand-to-hand I'd hoped for, but it was, one might say, spirit-to-spirit, and far from trivial. Thanks to Elena, I had my duel.

And I needn't comment on the worthiness of my adversary.

I was no Paris.

But Elena was now watching me in such a way that I wasn't sure just who I was anymore.

I knew that one day or another I would crack.

That day arrived.

It was — inevitably — in the spring, and even though the ghetto's flowers were ugly they were doing their job the best they could, like honest workers in an industrial commune.

There was something erotic in the air. The giant fans spread it everywhere.

Even in school.

It was a Friday. I hadn't set foot in school for a week because of a cold that I hoped might last till the weekend. In vain. I had tried mightily to convince my mother that the loss of an entire week of Pekingese education represented no significant intellectual loss, that I learned far more in bed reading the original translation of the *Arabian Nights*, and that I still felt weak. She didn't accept a word of it, and volleyed back that irksome argument:

"If you're still sick on Friday, I'll keep you in bed on Saturday and Sunday to make sure you get well again."

I could only submit and return to school on that Friday, a day that I didn't yet know was attributed to Venus by some, to the crucifixion by others, and to fire by others yet — none of which, with hindsight, seems inconsistent to me. In the course of my life, all three incarnations of Friday have appeared numerous times.

A long absence always has the effect of ennobling and excluding. The prestige of the illness isolated me a little, and I was able to concentrate better on making ever more sophisticated paper airplanes.

Recreation. The word is clear: it's about creating oneself over again. My experience, however, has proven the opposite: most kinds of recreation that I've taken part in have ended in destruction — and not necessarily someone else's.

But our recreation periods at school had always been sacred to me, because they allowed me to see Elena.

I had spent seven days without so much as a glimpse of her. Seven days is longer than it takes to create heaven and earth: it is eternity.

Eternity without my beloved had been a trial. Of course, my relations with her since revising my strategy had been limited to stolen glances, but these furtive glimpses were the most important things in my life: to see the face of the person one loves, particularly when that face is beautiful, is all it takes to choke an undernourished heart.

And mine was dying of hunger so that, like an starved cat who dares not eat, I dared not even look Elena in the eye. As I walked in the schoolyard, I kept my eyes on the ground.

Because of the still-recent thaw, the ground was a morass. I set each foot down cautiously on the firmer patches. It kept me occupied.

I saw two dainty feet approaching, delicately shod and stepping gracefully, ignoring the mud.

She gave me such a look! And she was so beautiful, with a beauty that filled my head with that idiotic leitmotif I mentioned earlier: "I must do something."

She asked, "Are you better now?"

An angel descending to visit her brother in hospital would have spoken no differently.

Better? You must be kidding.

"I'm okay."

"I missed you. I wanted to come and visit you but your mother said you were too sick."

Go have parents and see what it gets you! I tried all the same to turn this staggering news to my advantage:

"Yes," I said with grave detachment. "I almost died."

"Really?"

"It's happened before," I answered, shrugging my shoulders.

To have brushed elbows with death a number of times was like having one's own coat of arms and a host of noble relatives.

"Are we going to play together again?"

She, making proposals to me!

"We've never played together."

"You don't want to?"

"I've never wanted to."

Her voice was sad:

"That's not true. You used to want to. You don't love me any more."

At that point I had to leave immediately, or I would say something I'd wish I hadn't.

I spun on my heel and looked for the next dry place to step. I was in such a state that I couldn't distinguish the ground from the puddles.

I was trying to put my thoughts back together when Elena said my name.

For the very first time.

I was in an extraordinary state. I didn't even know if I liked it or not. My body froze from head to toe, a statue on a pedestal of mud.

The Italian girl walked 180 degrees around me, straight through everything, heedless of the fate of her elegant shoes. I found it painful to see her feet in the mud.

She stood in front of me.

The icing on the cake: she was crying.

"Why don't you love me any more?"

I don't know if she possessed the ability to cry on command. Be that as it may, her tears were most convincing.

She cried with consummate art: just a little, enough that it was not unattractive, huge eyes open so as not to mask any of that magnificent gaze, and to highlight the slow birth of each tear.

She didn't move an inch, she wanted me to sit through the whole show. Her face was perfectly immobile: she didn't even blink — as if she had cleared the stage of its scenery and cut the action of all supporting characters in order to spotlight the star turn.

Elena in tears: a contradiction in terms.

And I moved as little as she, and I stared into her eyes: it was as if we were waiting to see who would blink first. But the real contest in that mutual stare was much more profound.

I knew it was a battle but I didn't know the stakes — and I knew that Elena understood them, knew what she wanted and where she wanted me, and knew that I didn't know.

She fought well. She fought as if she had known me forever, as if she saw my weak points by X-ray. A lesser warrior would never have fixed me with that wounded expression, which would have caused any sane person to laugh but which pierced my poor, absurd heart.

I had till then read only two books: the Bible and the *Arabian Nights*. These books ought to be banned. They had infected me with a Middle Eastern sentimentality that I was already ashamed of.

Yet there I was, wrestling with the angel, and I had the impression I was giving as good an account of myself as Jacob. I hadn't blinked and my face betrayed nothing.

I don't know and I'll never know if Elena's tears were sincere. If I knew, I would now be able to determine whether what happened next was a master stroke on her part or mere luck.

Perhaps it was both, which is to say that she took a gamble.

She actually lowered her eyes.

It signified defeat far more strongly than blinking.

She lowered her head, as if emphasizing that she had lost.

In obedience to the laws of gravity, the inclination of her head emptied her lachrymal reserves, and I beheld two silent cascades rolling down her cheeks.

I had won. Believe me, such a victory was unbearable.

I began to speak. I said everything I shouldn't have said.

"Elena, I lied. I've been lying for months."

Two eyes returned to mine. I was astonished by their lack of astonishment: they simply waited.

It was too late.

"I love you. I never stopped loving you. I stopped looking at you because that was my strategy. But I watched you anyway, secretly, because I couldn't stop myself watching you, because you're so beautiful and because I love you."

A scourge less cruel than she would have already said something like, "You're just making it worse." Elena said nothing, and watched me with an almost medical interest. I was fully aware of that.

Mistakes are like alcohol: one very quickly becomes aware that one has gone too far but instead of having the wisdom to stop and limit the damage, a sort of rage takes over that has nothing to do with the alcohol itself. That bizarre fury might be called pride: the pride of declaring, over and against all objections, that one is right to drink and right to be wrong. To persist in one's error or in one's drinking becomes an argument in itself, a challenge to logic: if I hold fast to my position it's because I'm right, whatever anyone else thinks. And I'll hold fast until the elements have confirmed my position — I will become an alcoholic, I'll become a card-carrying member in the party of my error, waiting until I sink under the table or until people get bored with me; I will press on in the vague but aggressive hope of becoming the laughing stock of the entire world, convinced that in ten years, in ten centuries, Time or History or Legend will confirm I was right, which in any case makes no sense since Time validates everything; every error and every vice has its Golden Age, and being wrong is always a question of era.

In fact, those who cleave to their errors are mystics: they know, deep within themselves, that they have dug in for the long term, that they'll be dead long before History has validated their views, but they project themselves into the future with messianic emotion, convinced that they'll be remembered — that in the Century of Alcoholics people will say, "So-and-so, that indefatigable barfly, was a pioneer," and that during the Golden Age of Idiocy they'll have a religion devoted to them.

And so it was in March 1975, when I immediately realized that I'd made a mistake. And since I had the stuff of which true imbeciles are made, which is to say I had a sense of honor, I chose to dig myself in deeper:

"Now I'll stop pretending. Or maybe I won't, but you'll know that I'm pretending."

Now I had definitely gone too far.

Elena clearly found the situation had gone beyond a joke. She said with crushing indifference:

"That's all I wanted to know."

She turned around and walked unhurriedly away, her shoes barely sinking into the mud.

Though aware of my error, I couldn't bear the

result. The bill had come too quickly to my table: I hadn't even had time to savor my defeat.

I hopped clumsily through the muck in pursuit of the fair one.

"But Elena, don't you love me?"

She gave me a polite and absent look — a most eloquent answer — and continued to walk away.

It was like a slap across the face. My cheeks burned with anger, despair, and embarrassment.

Sometimes pride makes one lose one's dignity. When it comes on top of crazy and humiliated love, the disaster can escalate to terrible proportions.

With a leap, I caught up with my beloved.

"Oh no! That's too easy! If you're going to make me suffer, you have to watch me suffer!"

"Why? Is it interesting?" she said in her ermine tone.

"I don't care. You asked me to suffer, now you have to watch me suffer!"

"Did I ask you to do anything?" she said, neutral as Switzerland.

"How can you say such a thing?"

"Why are you talking so loudly? Do you want everyone to hear?"

"Yes, I do!"

"I see."

"I want everyone to know!"

"You want everyone to know that you are suffering and you want them to watch you suffer?"

"That's right!"

"Oh."

Her absolute indifference was inversely proportional to the rising interest of the other children in our little scene.

"Come back here! Look at me!"

She stopped and looked at me, patiently, the way one looks at some unfortunate creature who is about to perform his pathetic act.

"I want you to know and I want them to know. I love Elena, and I'll do whatever she asks, even if it kills me. Even if she doesn't care. When I had my asthma attack it was because Elena asked me to run till I dropped. She knew I had asthma and she knew I'd do whatever she said. She wanted me to sabotage myself, but she didn't know how far I would go. And she wants you to know all this. She wants me completely sabotaged."

The little kids didn't seem to understand what was going on, but the older ones did. Those who liked me watched horror-struck.

Elena looked at her pretty little watch.

"Recess is almost over. I'm going back to class," she said, the perfect child.

The spectators smiled. They seemed to find it rather funny. There may have been "only" about thirty or thirty-five, about a third of the school watching. It could have been worse.

And I'd carried out a terrific act of self-sabotage.

◆

My delirium lasted for about an hour. I felt an incomprehensible pride.

Then the pride faded very quickly.

By four o'clock, my memory of the morning's events filled me with deep worry.

That very night, I told my parents that I wanted to leave China as soon as possible.

"Join the club," said my father.

I almost answered, "Yes, but I'm the only one with a serious reason for leaving." I had the fortunate intuition to stifle that reply.

My brother and sister hadn't witnessed the affair. All they'd heard was that their little sister had put on a performance, which didn't bother them.

Soon after, my father learned he was being transferred to New York. I blessed Christopher Columbus.

But it wasn't to come until the summer.

I spent the few remaining months in disgrace. Actually, there was little need to feel ashamed: the children had forgotten my scene very quickly.

But Elena remembered. When her gaze met mine, its ironic distance crucified me.

One week before my family's departure, the war with the Nepalese had to stop.

This time the parents had nothing to do with it.

133

During a battle, one of the Nepalese pulled a knife from his pocket.

Up until then we had always fought with our bodies — and their contents. We had never used real weapons.

The effect of the blade was similar to that of the two atomic bombs dropped on Japan.

Our commander-in-chief did the unthinkable: he walked the length of the ghetto carrying a white flag.

Nepal accepted the peace offering.

We left China in the nick of time.

Going directly from Peking to New York upset my mental equilibrium.

My parents lost their common sense. They spoiled us children rotten. I adored it. I became an odious little brat.

Ten little girls at the Lycée Français in New York fell madly in love with me. I made them suffer abominably.

It was fabulous.

Two years ago the peregrinations of the diplomatic trade brought my father and Elena's father together at some social function in Tokyo.

Effusive compliments, memories of the "good old days" in Peking, the usual courtesies: "And your children, my dear fellow?"

In my father's rambling letter that followed, I learned that Elena had become a femme fatale. She was studying in Rome, and if no one had already killed himself over her, any number of people were threatening to do so.

The news put me in excellent humor.

Thank you, Elena, for teaching me all there is to know about love.

And bless you, Elena, for remaining true to your legend.

AFTERWORD

Loving Sabotage tells a true story: my own. I invented nothing, not even the names of the characters. Everything is true. Obviously I have no proof whatsoever. Go figure what, in the memory of a child of seven, belongs to reality or to the imagination. But that doesn't prevent me from affirming that everything is true in this novel.

Even so, there are witnesses: my brother, my sister —and especially the veritable Elena, who actually is named Elena and was such as I described her. Two years ago, on the occasion of the translation of this book in Italian, she read this story. Furious (why?), she called my Roman editor and demanded to meet me "to set a few things straight." I refused this meeting: there was nothing to set straight.

In French, an old proverb says: "It's only the truth that hurts." Elena's reaction could well be the proof that I invented nothing: if she was furious, it's because this story is true.

—Amélie Nothomb
March, 2000